THE TRUTH ABOUT THE VISCOUNT

WHISPERS OF THE TON (BOOK 4)

ROSE PEARSON

© Copyright 2025 by Rose Pearson - All rights reserved.

In no way is it legal to reproduce, duplicate, or transmit any part of this document by either electronic means or in printed format. Recording of this publication is strictly prohibited and any storage of this document is not allowed unless with written permission from the publisher. All rights reserved.

Respective author owns all copyrights not held by the publisher.

THE TRUTH ABOUT THE VISCOUNT

PROLOGUE

"Lord Hastings? I must speak with you."

Trying to recall the gentleman's name, Daniel Spearton, Viscount Hastings frowned, gesturing to where his sister was just about to make her way into the ballroom, their mother by her side.

"I am just about to watch Isabella step out into society, might this conversation wait?"

Tilting his head, he took in the gentleman's light frown, wishing that he could recall the gentleman's title.

"It is about your sister, Lord Hastings."

This gave Daniel pause. Earlier that day, Isabella had been presented to the King, and was now to enter her first ball of the Season, so what could have happened to make her of note to this gentleman?

"It is nothing to concern you, of course, only that I have to inform you of how captivated I have been by her beauty." The gentleman smiled warmly, his brown eyes turning to where Isabella now waited. "The reason I come to you with such urgency is in the hope that she might have been granted permission to waltz? I should not like to ask her to do so, only to realize that she has not been given such a thing. It would bring her embarrassment, and I should like to spare her that."

A little surprised at this request, Daniel's eyebrows lifted.

"I – I have not yet given her permission, no." Finally, the name of the gentleman came to him and Daniel frowned, remembering that the Earl of Newforth had not made the very best impression upon him during their introduction the previous year. Lord Newforth was loud, arrogant, and somewhat uncouth. Daniel was not at all certain that he wanted him near Isabella. "And, truth be told, I do not intend to give her permission for some time as yet."

Lord Newforth's face fell.

"That is disappointing."

Daniel lifted his chin just a little.

"All the same, that is my decision."

"And I quite understand." Lord Newforth grinned and slapped Daniel on the shoulder in a manner that spoke of familiarity, though Daniel did not feel at all closely acquainted with the fellow. "Then I shall ask her for another dance, I think. Mayhap the polka, or the country dance."

With a nod, he stepped away, leaving Daniel to narrow his eyes after him, reminding himself inwardly to warn Isabella to be cautious around Lord Newforth. There was something about the man that Daniel did not quite like, aside from his brashness. To pursue Isabella, to ask for the waltz from a young woman who was only just coming out, was much too forward in Daniel's eyes, and that in itself, was reason enough for his sister to be careful.

"Hastings?" His mother called to him, and Daniel,

pulling his gaze away from Lord Newforth, hurried to their side. "Your sister is waiting!"

"Yes, yes, I am well aware of that." Offering Isabella his arm, he smiled at her, seeing the nervousness dancing in her expression. "You have nothing to concern yourself with, my dear. The audience with the King went very well and now, you are to make your debut! I am sure that the *ton* will think very highly of you."

Isabella smiled at him, though it wobbled just a little.

"Thank you, brother."

"Though you are not to think of matrimony this Season," their mother reminded Isabella, making Daniel scowl. "You must remember that."

Daniel opened his mouth to protest but then closed it again, stepping forward into the busy ballroom instead. It was a conversation that they had shared before, but Daniel had not succeeded in getting his mother to change her opinion. Isabella was merely to enjoy this Season, it seemed, rather than pursue any hope of matrimony – and this, despite Daniel's insistence that it would be better for her to do quite the opposite!

"Oh, and I must ask you to be cautious around the Earl of Newforth, who will soon seek an introduction," he murmured into his sister's ear as they smiled and nodded to various acquaintances. "He appears to be quite fervent in his eagerness to meet you, but that does not mean that I think it wise."

Isabella's eyes rounded.

"Is there something wrong with his character?"

Daniel winced.

"Not that I can say specifically, my dear sister, but my heart warns me to be cautious there."

Isabella nodded.

"Then I shall do as you ask, my dear brother," she answered, taking a deep breath and then lifting her chin. "For I trust your judgment implicitly."

~

"The answer is no."

Daniel looked into Lord Newforth's eyes, gritting his teeth as shock poured into the Earl's expression.

"I – I beg your pardon?"

"No," Daniel repeated, a good deal more firmly this time. "No, Lord Newforth, I will not permit you to court my sister."

Lord Newforth blinked furiously, then pushed one hand through his hair. Clearly, this had not been the answer he was expecting from Daniel but, in the last fortnight, Daniel had found out a good deal more about Lord Newforth and his character, and he certainly was *not* about to let him court Isabella.

"I thought that we were well acquainted!" Lord Newforth flung up both hands as though he expected this to mean something to Daniel. "We have played cards together, have we not? Last evening, for example, we played for many an hour and–"

"And you owe me a great deal of money and instead, only gave me a vowel." Daniel lifted an eyebrow and waited for Lord Newforth to say something in response to this, to perhaps confirm that he intended to pay the debt very soon but, instead, the man only ignored Daniel's remark.

"You must know that my fervency regarding Isabella is genuine. In asking to court her, I have nothing on my mind but the intention to offer her my hand in marriage." Lord Newforth began to frown now, his jaw tightening as Daniel looked away. "Is there some reason that you refuse to let me court her? It is most unusual for there to be such a direct answer."

Daniel's lip curled. This in itself was an impertinence, for Lord Newforth ought not to be asking Daniel such a question. This was a matter entirely between Daniel and his family and, thus, for Lord Newforth to demand such a thing was more than rude. *Nor am I about to tell you the truth,* Daniel thought to himself, sniffing and then lifting his chin.

"Lord Newforth, I have decided that my sister shall not even consider matrimony this Season."

"Oh?" Lord Newforth's eyes sharpened. "Why would a gentleman do such a thing?"

Anger shot through Daniel's frame.

"Lord Newforth, it is not proper for you to ask me such a thing. Isabella is my sister and therefore, I have decided what is best for her, and I need not share my reasoning with you! All I am here to tell you is that your request to court her is not going to be accepted."

"Then next Season?" Lord Newforth put both hands behind his back, a smile on his face that brought no light into his eyes. "You will let me court her next Season?"

All the more frustrated, Daniel shook his head.

"No, Lord Newforth. I will not." The truth began to burn in his heart and threw itself up into his throat. "Lord Newforth, I have heard of, and now know of, your character and it is not one that would bring my sister any joy. In addition, I have been warned about your lack of consideration for others, your inclination towards gambling and, to be blunt, your desire to call upon ladies of the night with great frequency. That is not the sort of gentleman I would ever consider suitable for my sister."

He watched as Lord Newforth's chin began to lift, his eyes narrowing, a red flush beginning to spread up into his face.

"How dare you?" Lord Newforth took a step closer to Daniel, scarlet in his cheeks now. "There is more to my character than what you have stated!"

"But what I have said of you is true, all the same." Unmoved, Daniel fought to keep his voice level, refusing to respond to Lord Newforth's anger. "Now, if you will excuse me, Lord Newforth, this conversation is at an end."

"No!" Lord Newforth shook one finger in Daniel's face, his eyes like fire. "You cannot deny me!"

A little astonished at this statement, Daniel reared back, wondering if this was the first time that anyone had ever denied Lord Newforth something that he desired.

"I believe that I can," he said, ringing the bell quickly so that the butler might open the door. "And I have. As I have said, Lord Newforth, it is time for you to take your leave. Good afternoon."

What came as Lord Newforth's answer was some furious breaths, a glaring of his eyes into Daniel's, and a jaw which was gritted tight but, much to Daniel's relief, he finally swung around and made his way to the now open door. The butler closed it quickly after him and Daniel, once more left alone, finally let himself slump down into a chair.

That was most unexpected.

Letting out a low whistle of surprise, Daniel blinked quickly, then rubbed one hand over his jaw. It was clear to him that he had made the right decision when it came to Lord Newforth's intentions towards Isabella, and that was a great relief.

All Daniel could do now was pray that come the

following Season, Lord Newforth would know not to try again, for Daniel had every intention of refusing him should he so much as glance in Isabella's direction – and perhaps, next time, with even greater force than had been required today.

"You shall not have her," he muttered aloud, as though Lord Newforth could hear him. "I promise you that, Newforth. You shall never succeed in your attempt to wed my sister."

CHAPTER ONE

"And so we now come to the Season."

Daniel grinned and took the glass of brandy from his friend Samuel, the Viscount of Milthorpe.

"We do indeed!"

"And this time, will you permit your sister to wed?"

At this, Daniel rolled his eyes.

"I do not know *why* my mother insisted that she wait. Last Season would have been the perfect time for her to secure a match but no, it was not to be." With a sigh, he shook his head. "It seems that this Season, I must do my duty as I did last Season and shall not have the chance to do as I please until she is wed!"

"Your mother is present also, yes?"

Daniel nodded.

"Yes, she is. Though she is not present this evening, for she is a little weary from traveling still."

His friend chuckled.

"Then you must do all that you can to marry your sister to a respectable gentleman just as soon as possible, for then you shall have all the freedom that you desire."

Daniel laughed aloud before throwing back his brandy and, thereafter, picking up another from the tray of a passing footman.

"Though I must say, I shall still be careful when it comes to Isabella's husband." Growing suddenly serious, he waggled one finger in Lord Milthorpe's direction. "You must not encourage me to push her into the arms of the very first gentleman who seeks to court her, for I certainly will *not* do such a thing as that."

Thankfully, Lord Milthorpe did not take the least bit of offense, though he did hold up both hands, palms out towards Daniel.

"I shall not do so."

"You recall the conversation that I had with Lord Newforth last Season?" Daniel scowled at the memory of it. "That gentleman was most insistent that he be the one to court Isabella with the prospect of marriage in his view, but hearing of his character, I had no choice but to refuse him. I care about her a great deal, though I jest about my lack of freedom and the like. She must have a suitable husband, who is good in both his temperament and his standing."

Lord Milthorpe put one hand to his heart.

"I swear to you that I shall do all that I can to support you in this."

"I thank you."

"Though, if I recall, did you make it quite clear last Season that your sister was *not* to marry?"

Frowning gently, Daniel nodded.

"I did."

"Then might I give you a warning?" Lord Milthorpe continued, coming a little closer and, thereafter, gesturing to the crowd around them. "The *ton* know of your wealth, Daniel. They know that your sister will have an excellent dowry, and a fine income thereafter. You must be on your guard, my dear friend, for there will be many a gentleman who might well seek her out based on her fortune."

Daniel scowled darkly, looking around the crowd as his friend did, wondering which of these gentlemen might do such a thing as that. It was not a thought that he had given much time to consider, but now that Lord Milthorpe had said it, Daniel could well understand it.

"I value your considerations, my friend." His scowl grew darker. "It is something which I have thought upon for myself, I will admit, but I did not consider it for my sister."

Daniel's wealth was great indeed, even greater than those with higher titles and while he was very careful indeed to push away any young ladies – or their grasping mothers – from his company, he had not thought that such a thing could happen to Isabella. That, he saw, had been an oversight. Irritated still by his lack of consideration and, in addition, the realization of how selfish some of the *ton* could be, Daniel finished up his second brandy and then reached for a third.

"Another?"

Seeing Lord Milthorpe's slightly lifted eyebrow, Daniel shrugged.

"I must try to enjoy myself a little, must I not?"

His friend hesitated for a moment, then looked away.

"I suppose so."

"Do not worry." Daniel waved one hand vaguely. "I know my responsibilities this evening, and I will not forget them."

∽

"Lord Hastings?"

Turning a little too quickly, Daniel blinked to clear his vision.

"Ah, Lady Winters."

He wobbled just a little, one hand reaching out to hold onto the chair beside him though, somehow, it seemed to evade his grasp.

"Have you seen my daughter?" Lady Winters' eyes were wide with concern and Daniel quickly forced his smile away. "She was dancing with Lord Beauford and now I cannot see her anywhere!"

"I am sure that she is quite all right," Daniel answered, setting his brandy down rather than taking another sip, seeing that Lady Winters required his full attention. "She mayhap was dancing the cotillion, yes? And that dance has only just been announced."

Lady Winters wrung her hands.

"No, no, I am sure that she did not accept that dance from anyone! I do not know where she has gone and yet now, I fear that her reputation might well be in danger if I do not find her soon."

Daniel turned quickly and grasped the arm of his friend.

"Lord Milthorpe, come for a moment. It appears that Lady Winters requires our aid."

"And your discretion!" Lady Winters exclaimed as Daniel threw a glance at the glass of very fine French brandy that he might otherwise have been enjoying. "I came to speak with you, Lord Hastings, because I know that you are not in the *least* bit inclined towards gossip and are a fine, upstanding gentleman."

Her eyes glittered with evident tears as Daniel nodded, his chest puffed out a little with pride at the compliments the lady had offered him.

"You can be quite assured that we will not say a single thing, Lady Winters," he said firmly, feeling the effects of the liquor slowly beginning to fade, though it still slung to him quite firmly, loosening its grip bit by bit. "We must find Lady..."

A heavy frown pulled at his forehead as he struggled to recall the name of the young lady, although he was well able to picture her face. Lady Winter scowled.

"Lady Madeline."

"Yes, yes, of course." Daniel shook his head, flushed with embarrassment. "Forgive me, it is only that there are so many names and those eager to dance that I quite forgot for a moment."

He smiled as warmly as he could, and Lady Winters gave him a brief nod before wringing her hands again.

"Oh, where could she be?" Her eyes flared suddenly. "Wait! Might she be with your sister?"

Daniel blinked quickly.

"My sister?" Again, heat poured into his chest as he realized that he had not seen sight nor sound of Isabella for some time. "Yes, mayhap. I know that they are acquainted, but I did not think that they would consider one another a friend."

"Oh, but they do!" Lady Winters exclaimed, her eyes darting from Daniel to Lord Milthorpe and then back again. "Last Season, they were often in conversation, and I am sure that letters have been exchanged since then also."

"I see."

Daniel cleared his throat, reaching for his brandy only to set it back again. He had not known this and though he realized that, mayhap, he did not know his sister as well as he ought, he certainly had never *seen* Isabella in conversation with Lady Madeline.

"Might I ask where your sister is, Lord Hastings?" Lady Winters came closer to him, one hand on his arm. "We might go and find them together!"

Daniel glanced around the room, trying to find an answer to Lady Winters' question.

"I think..." Realizing that he had failed in his duty to his sister, he drew himself up and nodded vaguely in the direction of the center of the ballroom. "She was dancing, Lady Winters. I think she will be in the middle of the cotillion at present."

"Oh." Lady Winters let out a long sigh. "Then she will not be with my dear daughter." Squeezing Daniel's arm again, she caught his full attention. "Might you still be willing to seek out Madeline with me?"

Daniel cleared his throat but smiled.

"Yes, of course. I am honored that you would ask me." He looked at his friend. "Lord Milthorpe?"

"Oh, I do not think that your friend needs to be troubled." Lady Winters smiled, but put one hand out toward Lord Milthorpe. "Please, do not think that you must join us. I should not like to impose."

A trifle confused as to why Lady Winters would not want as much help and assistance as she could get, Daniel threw a look at his friend again.

"It is no trouble in the least, I assure you." Lord Milthorpe gestured to the door that led from the ballroom. "Shall we see if she is in the hallway? There might be a ripped gown that requires stitching or mayhap she has stepped out for a little air."

"Then the gardens?" Lady Winters took Daniel's arm, even though he had not offered it, and then hurried them both towards the French doors, rather than the one that led out to the hallway. "I am sure that she would not have gone out to the gardens alone but, all the same, it might be wise to make certain."

"Indeed."

Becoming a little more confused as to why Lady Winters appeared to be so determined to have him out in the gardens, Daniel cast another look over his shoulder to Lord Milthorpe who was frowning heavily. The cold air sent a slight shock through him and Daniel blinked rapidly, astonished at the way the night air pushed away the slowness that came from the sheer amount of brandy he had indulged in.

"Do you think that we should call for her?" Lady Winters looked up into Daniel's face, the flickers from the many torches lighting the garden dancing across her features. "But then that might make others aware that she is lost, and I do not want that."

"No, I should not do such a thing as that." Trying to quieten his thoughts over what Lady Winters appeared to be doing in practically dragging him outside, Daniel turned his gaze around the gardens but much of it was dark and hidden in shadow. "We should walk through the gardens quietly and see if we can see her anywhere. I am sure that she is merely standing with some companions and will be most apologetic over her absence from you."

"I will go this way." Lord Milthorpe took the path to the left and, with a nod, Daniel turned to the right. The gardens were large enough for many to walk in, though quite why a young lady would come out here alone, Daniel could not imagine. He walked in silence with Lady Winters, hearing only her quick breaths and practically sensing her concern.

Then, Daniel heard someone cry out and his heart lurched at the sound. Before he could say anything, Lady

Winters released his arm and rushed forward into the darkness, leaving Daniel to follow her.

"Lady Winters, a moment!" Following her behind some bushes – his concern growing that *he* might soon be caught alone with Lady Winters herself and some questions raised thereafter – Daniel moved slowly, silently wondering now if this had all been some foolish mistake on his part. Mayhap he ought never to have come outside or even agreed to assist her in this! "I do not think–"

"Goodness, Lord Hastings! Is that not... your sister?"

Daniel snatched in a breath, his eyes flaring as a flaming torch on a marble plinth illuminated the two figures before them. One of them was being held, her wrists tightly gripped, pressed back against the tree, and the other, he could not quite make out, given that the gentleman had his back to him. Before he could even think, Daniel strode forward across the grass and grasped the gentleman's shoulder with one hand, wrenching him back just as his sister let out another cry, trying to fight Daniel off also.

"Isabella, it is I!" he exclaimed, only for her to break into sobs, throwing herself into his arms. She went a little limp, perhaps weak with fright, over what had taken place and Daniel, turning carefully, looked into the face of the gentleman who had held his sister so tightly.

"How dare you?" Taking a step closer, one arm still around Isabella's waist, he fought the furious anger that burned up into his chest, threatening to overwhelm him. "Did you really think that this was the right way for a gentleman to behave towards a lady he supposedly cares for, Lord Newforth?"

Much to Daniel's upset, the gentleman only smiled, grinning back at Daniel as though he had done something quite acceptable.

"Hastings?" A rush of footsteps brought Lord Milthorpe to stand beside Daniel, and then, quickly taking in the scene, he moved to stand on the opposite side of Isabella. "Whatever has happened here?"

"Oh, it is quite clear." Lady Winters, suddenly no longer appearing as sorrowful nor as afraid as before, came to stand beside Lord Newforth. "I have discovered your sister, Isabella, in the arms of Lord Newforth. I am afraid that they must now wed, given the circumstances."

Cold ran down Daniel's spine and he shuddered violently.

"Never," he hissed, his arm around Isabella gripping her a little more tightly. "I shall never permit you to wed her!"

"Ah, but the *ton* shall then know all that has taken place!" Lord Newforth exclaimed, throwing one hand out towards Lady Winters. "My aunt is not known for her quiet tongue, I am afraid."

"Your *aunt*?" Closing his eyes, Daniel let out a hiss of breath, quickly realizing what had just taken place. Lord Newforth, for whatever reason, desired to have Isabella as his bride and thus, had used his aunt to force Daniel's hand. If he refused to let Isabella marry Lord Newforth, then her reputation would be utterly ruined, and all that he had hoped for her would fade into nothing. Even his good name would be damaged, and that meant that any match he might hope to make would be a good deal more difficult. And what would his mother think of it all? He opened his eyes and turned to Isabella, seeing the tears on her cheeks, and feeling her tremble still. Twisting his lips, he shook his head. "I cannot do this to her. The answer is no."

Lady Winters laughed mockingly.

"Then you do realize what you are going to face, do you not?"

"Mockery," Lord Newforth began, ticking his fingers off one by one. "Disdain. The cut direct from many, I am sure. Gossip. Whispers. No longer invited to the fine events held in society." He tilted his head, one eyebrow lifting just a little. "Is that really what you want? What you want for *her*?" His eyes went to Isabella, a darkness coming into them that Daniel shuddered to see. "Or do you not wish to encourage her to marry me and, in doing so, save yourself – and her – from all that I have said before?"

"You cannot." Lord Milthorpe turned his head to look straight into Daniel's face, his expression furious. "You cannot let him do this."

"There is truth in what he says, however," Daniel murmured, only for Isabella to let out a low cry, her hands now grasping his arm.

"Do not make me wed him, brother, I beg you! You know the character that he is, please do not force me into his arms!"

Daniel took a deep breath, seeing the fear in his sister's face, but at the same time, struggling to know what would be best to do. He wanted to protect her but, no matter what decision he made, she would suffer.

"I will marry her." Lord Milthorpe turned his back on Lord Newforth and Lady Winters, his voice low but determined.

"I beg your pardon?"

In response to Daniel's question, Lord Milthorpe repeated himself, albeit more firmly.

"*I* will marry Isabella. We can make the announcement at this very moment and prevent any gossip from spreading."

Daniel swallowed hard, looking from his sister to Lord Milthorpe and back again. Isabella's eyes were shining with tears, but Lord Milthorpe appeared quite resolute, his jaw tight as he nodded, as though to confirm that he would do as he had just said.

"We are awaiting your decision, Lord Hastings!"

The droll, almost sing-song voice of Lord Newforth made Daniel's whole body clench with anger, and he almost turned around on his heel to throw something sharp in the gentleman's direction, though Isabella's restraining hand prevented him.

"I will marry Lord Milthorpe."

Her whisper shattered Daniel's heart, seeing the sorrow in his sister's eyes that she would not have the Season – nor the match - she had hoped for.

"This is my fault, my doing." Guilt began to tear through him, making him lower his head. "I should have made certain that I knew where you were at all times, should have come to find you after the dance."

"Now is not the time for such things." Lord Milthorpe moved a little closer, keeping his voice low. "I know that I am not the very best of gentlemen, but you know my character well enough to trust that I will treat Isabella with every kindness." He looked at Isabella as Daniel watched, his expression softening. "We have known each other from childhood, have we not? I am sure that we can make the best of things, and I swear to treat you with the greatest consideration, Isabella."

For just a moment, Isabella's lips lifted in a small smile, a flare of hope in her eyes.

"I do trust you in that, Milthorpe. Thank you for saving me from this dreadful situation."

Seeing that both had already made up their minds and, fully aware that this was now the very best that could be made of the situation, Daniel took a deep breath, nodded, and then looked at Lord Newforth.

"The answer is no, Lord Newforth, just as I have said before, and now say again. You will *not* have my sister as your wife."

The light smile on Lord Newforth's face immediately began to fade away. He exchanged a look with Lady Winters who, at the very same time, began to scowl.

"You know what this will mean, then," she spat, clearly disappointed and angry that Daniel had refused. "We will tell everyone–"

"Do excuse me." Interrupting her and making it quite clear that he had no interest whatsoever in listening to anything further, Daniel marched away from both Lady Winters and Lord Newforth, following Isabella and Lord Milthorpe. His chest was tight, filled with furious anger that he could not quite remove from himself and, at the very same time, guilt and shame ran over him in waves. He had been doing nothing but enjoying himself at the ball and had not given Isabella the attention that she deserved and required from him. Had he done so, then Lord Newforth might never have had the opportunity to do as he had done.

Stepping into the ballroom, he paused at the door, hearing Lord Milthorpe call for quiet. It took some moments as the hush slowly ran around the room but, after a short while, almost everyone had paused in their conversation and was now looking directly at him.

Lord Milthorpe smiled, though Daniel could see the slight flicker in it all the same. Lord Milthorpe had done more for Daniel and Isabella than Daniel had ever expected, saving her from a life of ruination or a life of pain with Lord Newforth – and Daniel did not know how he would ever express his gratitude.

"I am delighted to announce that I have only just now asked Miss Isabella Spearton, sister to the Viscount of Hastings, to be my wife. What is even more wonderful is that she has accepted and, very soon, we shall wed!"

"What?"

Daniel turned, just as the room erupted with applause and cheers. The first thing that met his eyes was the sight of Lord Newforth, now rigid with fury, his eyes narrowed like shards of glass, his whole face scarlet with rage.

Despite all else that he felt, Daniel smiled.

"I did tell you that you would not marry my sister, did I not?" he said, as calmly as he could. "And now you may speak whatever you please, but I highly doubt that anyone in society will believe you. Instead, it will appear as though you are either jealous, idiotic, or mistaken." His shoulders lifted and then fell. "But I shall leave that choice to you."

Turning back, he walked directly towards his sister, forcing a smile that he did not truly feel within himself. The moment was done, the decision was made, and Daniel had no choice but to go with it wholeheartedly. He could only pray that Isabella would be happy with Lord Milthorpe... and that she would forgive him for his failure.

CHAPTER TWO

"Is that not wonderful?"
Lady Patience Tynan smiled at her sister's words.

"It is a lovely announcement, certainly." Her smile slipped just a little as she took in the young lady, seeing the slight wobble of her lips and the paleness of her cheeks. "I do hope that she is happy about her betrothal."

"Miss Spearton?"

A little surprised, Patience turned to her sister.

"You are acquainted with the lady?"

Christina nodded.

"Yes, we were introduced earlier this evening."

"I see." Patience tilted her head a little, studying the young lady. "It may be that she is a little unsure of the amount of attention now being pushed upon her. Perhaps she did not expect Lord Milthorpe to make such a big announcement!"

Her sister smiled, letting out a soft sigh as she did so.

"Ah, but is it not a beautiful thing to have a gentleman

so enamored of his lady, to be so delighted at her acceptance, that he cannot help but declare it to all?"

With a quiet smile, Patience looked away, a gentle longing coming into her heart. Yes, she had to admit, that would be quite wonderful and was something that she longed for. Whether she would ever be able to find a gentleman who might care for her with such consideration and passion, she did not know, but the hope remained, all the same.

"Now, my dears, who is it that you are to dance with next?"

Patience smiled at her mother.

"I have the next dance free, Mama."

Lady Osterley's eyes flared, her mouth rounding into a small circle for a moment.

"No, no!" she exclaimed, flapping one hand wildly in Patience's direction. "You must find someone to stand up with at once! This will not do! You must be seen to dance every dance and–"

"Mama, please." Christina cast a look at Patience, a wry smile on her lips, before settling one hand on Lady Osterley's arm. "You must not be so concerned. This is only our third ball of the Season, and you know as well as I that all has gone very well up until this moment! Patience does not have to dance every dance for her to be noticed, just as I do not. Recall, I did not have *two* dances filled on my card at Lord and Lady Smythe's ball and I still had gentlemen coming to call the following day."

At this, Lady Osterley blinked rapidly, then seemed to shrink just a little as though the wave of anxiety that had buoyed her had finally started to fade away.

"Very well, very well." She patted Christina's hand,

then looked out at the crowd. "It is only that I want very much for you *both* to be in such a position, very soon."

Patience shared another smile with Christina, both of them very aware of their mother's fervent desire for them both to wed. It had been unfortunate that Patience had been unable to make her come out last Season – their father's travels to the continent had prevented it – and thus, it had been decided that both she and Christina would make their come out together this Season. Having been presented only the previous week, both Patience and Christina were doing their best to settle into society, to understand its twists and turns whilst, at the same time, battling a mother who was quite insistent on pushing them both as far into society as she could! Patience well understood her mother's urgency, for her father, the Earl of Osterley, was back at the estate, preparing to make his way to the continent again, and thus the desire was great for them both to wed before his journey commenced.

"Well, at least we know that Lord Milthorpe is not a gentleman worth considering," Patience smiled, as Christina laughed softly, though Lady Osterley only frowned. "Now, Christina, are you not to dance this evening?"

"I am." Christina turned her head, looking around. "I think that the dance has been a little delayed thanks to Lord Milthorpe's announcement, but Lord Jeffries should be here any moment."

Lady Osterley frowned.

"A Viscount?"

"Yes, Mama, a Viscount," Christina answered as Patience hid a smile. "You know very well that what is important to me is the gentleman's character, *not* his title."

Knowing that this would bring mother and daughter

into a sharp disagreement – one that Patience hoped they would both keep as quiet as they could – Patience stepped a little away from them, choosing not to remain a part of the conversation. Their mother was so very eager for Patience and Christina to wed, yes, but she was also most determined about *which* sort of gentlemen would be suitable. It was not, under any circumstances, to be a gentleman with a lower title than their father's, she had insisted, though Christina and Patience had both *also* insisted that they cared very little for such things. A gentleman might have one of the highest titles in all of England, but still be an utter wretch, whereas another fellow might bear only a lowly title but have nothing but goodness within him.

I know very well which sort of gentleman I might wish to marry.

Smiling to herself, Patience leaned against one of the tall pillars in the room, letting herself simply observe. This was one of her greatest delights in life, simply watching those around her so that she could store their images in her mind. Thereafter, she would sit and draw what she remembered, bringing the gentlemen and ladies she had seen to life on the page... though, often, their features could be a little exaggerated! It brought her a good deal of contentment although, of course, she had been forced to promise her mother that she would not let any of the *ton* know that she enjoyed such a pastime, for fear that there would be some who might feel insulted by her drawings.

Who shall I draw next?

A light smile on her face, Patience let her gaze wander over the crowd. She took in Lord Milthorpe and his betrothed, seeing them speaking together with their heads close to one another. Ignoring the slight pang in her heart at the way that they stood so closely together, she studied them for a long moment, taking in their faces, their expressions, and the stance of each. A small smile touched the edges of her lips. Yes, *this* would be her next sketch – she could only hope that she would do them justice!

With that smile still lingering, Patience's gaze roved to the left, only to be caught by another gentleman. He too was looking at Lord Milthorpe and his betrothed, though Patience could not quite make out the expression on his face. It was somewhere between agony and happiness, a darkness shadowing his features but a tiny smile gracing his lips. What was this, now? Was it a gentleman sorrowful over the loss of Miss Spearton from society? Had he too been hopeful of pursuing a match with her, only to then hear Lord Milthorpe declare his intentions? Was it that, though he felt that pain, he was also glad that the lady had found a good match? A little intrigued, Patience continued to watch the fellow, taking in the shock of dark hair that cast itself over his forehead, swept lightly to one side though it still fell carelessly all the same. There was a firm jaw, a long, straight nose, and lips which looked as though they were more inclined towards laughter than scowling, though at this moment it did appear as though he was quite uncertain as to which he wanted to do.

Her eyebrows lifted as he suddenly straightened to his full height and, thereafter, made his way directly toward the young lady and Lord Milthorpe. A slight tug in Patience's stomach spoke of curiosity and warning, and she was afraid now that he might do something impetuous and ruin Miss Spearton's happy moment... but her fears were for naught. Much to her surprise, not only did he shake Lord Milthorpe's hand, but he put one arm around Miss Spearton's waist, and the young lady, thereafter, leaned her head on his shoulder.

How very curious.

"You are looking at Lord Hastings, I see."

Patience started in surprise, an excuse ready on her lips, only to see a familiar face smiling at her.

"Eleanor! Good evening, how wonderful it is to see you!" Embracing her cousin and dear friend, she grasped Eleanor's hands. "I did not think that you would be at the ball this evening. Is not your come out tomorrow?"

Eleanor shook her head.

"When last I wrote to you, I thought it was to be tomorrow, but I was quite wrong." She laughed, a little ruefully. "You know as well as I that I am often inclined towards forgetfulness and confusion, am I not?"

"You should have written to me again and I would have attended."

"I would have liked that, but there was no time. Mama was *very* determined to have me do nothing other than sit and wait in silence until my gown arrived, I think for fear that I might wander off and do something quite ridiculous."

Patience giggled, her arm slipping through Eleanor's.

"Well, you have been inclined towards such things, have you not?"

Her own mother and Eleanor's mother, the Countess of Pearson, were sisters and were, also, of the same inclinations as regarded their characters. Both could be rather anxious and fretted a good deal about their daughters. Patience and Christina had done what they could to quieten their mother's concerns, whereas Eleanor had done quite the opposite. Shunning her mother's stranglehold, she had often been found riding wildly across the estate grounds, climbing trees, or swimming in the lake – and Patience, when she had visited, had been inclined to join her. Now, however, she could quite understand why Lady Pearson wished Eleanor to do nothing other than sit quietly in a place where she might be not only seen but contained. That way, she could be quite certain that her daughter would not ruin her gown, or damage herself in some way or another before her come out.

"And as I was saying, you are watching Lord Hastings?" Eleanor's eyes twinkled. "Yes, you must wonder how I am acquainted with him but, alas, I am not. Though I do think him *very* handsome."

Patience giggled again, seeing how Eleanor grinned at her, clearly waiting for her to agree.

"I shall admit that he is handsome, yes, though there are many handsome gentlemen here this evening, are there not?"

"There are." Eleanor gestured to the gentleman in question, though Patience pulled her hand down quickly for fear the action would be noticed. "He is brother to Miss Spearton, you understand? And Lord Milthorpe is Lord Hastings' very dear friend, so it is not too great a surprise to the *ton* that they are now betrothed."

Her eyebrows lifting, Patience gave her cousin a long look and Eleanor laughed immediately.

"I have been eavesdropping," she confessed, as Patience laughed aloud. "I stood near three young ladies when Lord Milthorpe made his announcement and found out all that I have just said to you, merely by listening! And then I saw you watching him and thought that I would take advantage of my newfound knowledge by sharing it with you." Her eyes twinkled brightly. "Might I ask if you intend to draw Lord Hastings? He would make a good subject, I am sure."

Patience smiled.

"I thought I would draw Lord Milthorpe and Miss

Spearton first," she answered. "Thereafter, I might consider Lord Hastings. I am not yet sure."

"Well, do promise me that you shall let me see the works when you have completed them?"

With a nod, Patience promised that she would do so, her fingers suddenly itching to put pencil to paper once more.

CHAPTER THREE

"Isabella?" There was something like relief in Daniel's heart as his sister offered him a welcoming smile as he came into the room. It had been three days since the incident with his sister and Lord Newforth, and Daniel had not wanted to approach her to speak about anything until he was quite sure she was ready. Today, however, looked to be the day, given the slight color in her cheeks and the warmth in her expression. "Isabella, I did wonder if we might speak together?"

"You wish to talk about my betrothal?"

Daniel nodded and came to sit down, only to then rise again to ring the bell so that they both might enjoy a little refreshment.

"Mama will soon come to join us, I am sure, though I would like to have a few moments alone with you first."

"I am not distressed if that is your concern."

Daniel shook his head.

"It is not that, Isabella, though I am glad to hear you say it. The reason I wanted to speak with you is so that I might apologize for my lack of consideration, and my failure in my responsibility to you." Isabella's eyebrows lifted. "I – I should have made certain to find you once that dance was at an end," Daniel began, the heaviness that had been in his heart since that evening now beginning to weigh him down all the more. "I did not. I was enjoying my brandy and to be truthful, Isabella, I quite forgot that our mother was not with us and that I had the sole responsibility for you." Isabella pressed her lips tight together and then turned her head away, as though there was something she wished to say but could not quite be sure how to go about it. "I was wrong to do such a thing," Daniel continued his breath tight in his chest now. "I have only myself to blame but, what troubles me the most, is that *you* have suffered the consequences of my failure."

"Oh, Hastings." Isabella shook her head, then looked back at him, her eyes damp. "I will not disagree with you, but I will *also* say that Lord Newforth surprised me utterly. He took my arm and led me from the ballroom so quickly, and in such a crowd of people also, that I quite lost myself in astonishment – to the point that I did not even cry out! When he marched me through the gardens, I did begin to exclaim, but he hissed in my ear that if I were to make a single sound of protest, then all of the other guests would hear me, and would, thereafter, wonder what I was doing in the arms of a gentleman without my brother's company. I did not know what to do, nor what his intentions were, and thus, I remained silent."

"I think that was the best thing for you to do, given the circumstances," Daniel answered, his heart still filled with a great deal of pain and regret over what he had done. "I should have been more watchful, Isabella. I should have stayed near to the dance floor and never once taken my eyes from you."

Isabella reached out one hand and settled it over his, just as the tea tray was brought in. She said nothing until the maid had left the room, though tears still burned in her eyes and Daniel's heart tore with what he had done to her.

"You are not to break yourself apart over this, Hastings." Isabella squeezed his hand lightly and then rose to her feet, going to pour the tea. "I can see that you are deeply sorrowful over what has happened, but I want now to focus on my future, and on what is to take place."

"Lord Milthorpe will be a good husband," Daniel answered, though he too rose to his feet, his hands clasping behind his back. "But I know that you did not want this sort of connection, you wanted very much to make your own match. I am sorry, truly sorry, that you have had that chance taken from you."

"Lord Milthorpe has promised to do all that he can to care for me, and I believe his words," Isabella answered, clearly choosing not to say anything in response to what Daniel had said. "He does care for me, and I for him."

"But not with the type of affection that I know you had hoped for," Daniel answered, a little woeful now, as Isabella handed him his cup of tea. "There is care and consideration between you, yes, but that is only because you have known each other for so very long."

"And yet, that may well be an advantage," came the answer. "We can build on our friendship and knowledge of each other to make a happy and contented marriage." Perhaps seeing that Daniel was about to speak again, Isabella held out one hand to him, taking his own and then pressing it gently. "You are right, it is not as I might have wished it, but at the same time, I will not complain, nor protest that Lord Milthorpe is to be my husband. He is a good man, with a kind heart and a loyalty that is clear to both myself and to others who have known him. Your friendship with him speaks of that. Yes, he might not have been my choice, but he is a *good* choice."

The door opened before Daniel could answer, their mother coming through the door to join them, though her eyes went from Daniel and then Isabella before returning to Daniel again.

"My dear children." She smiled, though Daniel could see the concern in her eyes. "How do you fare today?"

"I am well, Mama." Isabella smiled in response and then gestured to the tea tray. "Would you like to take something with us?"

Nodding, Lady Hastings sat down and then looked at Daniel.

"Are you well, my son?"

Daniel tried to nod, tried to say that he was quite contented, only for the words to stick in his throat. Instead, he simply shrugged and then sat back down, his teacup still in his hand. He had not told his mother everything that had taken place, had merely informed her that Lord Milthorpe had asked for Isabella's hand and that he had given his consent, so long as Isabella herself was contented. His mother, Daniel was sure, had not merely accepted that explanation, however, for it was clear both to herself and Daniel that something more was not being said.

"You are not as happy as I thought you might be over your sister's betrothal," Lady Hastings continued when Daniel did not answer. "Is it because she is to wed your very dear friend? I am sure that it will make things even better for all of you."

Forcing a smile, Daniel nodded.

"I am certain that you are quite correct in that. It came

about very quickly, Mother, which accounts for my surprise. That is all."

"It was rather surprising, yes." Lady Hastings switched her gaze from Daniel to her daughter instead. "It must have been something of an astonishment to you also, my dear. Though you do seem to be happy."

Isabella looked down at her teacup and then lifted her shoulders just a little.

"It was unexpected. I did not expect Lord Milthorpe to offer for my hand, but he was so very fervent in his desire that I could not help but accept him. I do know him very well, since we are childhood friends, and I trust that we will have a happy marriage."

"And that is why you accepted him?" Lady Hastings studied her daughter carefully, curiosity in her voice and expression. "I did think that you wanted to make your own choice in this, that you were glad to have been given another Season so that you might choose for yourself."

Daniel opened his mouth, ready to tell his mother all as he shifted uncomfortably in his chair.

"Mother, I–"

"I think that I realized how good a choice he would be." Isabella interrupted Daniel in a somewhat loud voice, making their mother's eyebrows lift in surprise. "Sometimes, Mama, it seems to me a little overwhelming to realize just how much is required in choosing a husband. I understand that society often presents gentlemen in a very different way from how they truly are, and gentlemen themselves can pretend to be what they are not, to secure a bride." She shook her head and sighed. "Besides which, I know that I have an excellent dowry and a fortune to come to me yearly thereafter, so I understand that even that might have caused me some difficulty when it came to ensuring that all of the gentlemen who wished to court me were just as they said they were!"

Daniel looked away, aware that his sister was doing what she could to defend him, to silence him so that he would not have to explain himself to their mother, and yet, the urge to tell her everything was still present. He shot a look at Isabella, but she gave him a small shake of her head, clearly telling him to remain silent.

"Well, I do think that the match is a good one, but so long as you are happy, Isabella." Lady Hastings glanced from Isabella to Daniel and then back again. "Just so long as nothing untoward has taken place, which has forced this match."

Again, the urge to tell all rose within Daniel's heart, but it was Isabella who spoke next.

"Please, Mama, there is no need to concern yourself with such thoughts! You think well of Lord Milthorpe, do you not?" When their mother nodded, Isabella's warm smile returned. "Then be assured that all is well and that I am quite contented with Lord Milthorpe." She set her teacup down. "Now, shall we think about my trousseau?"

Instantly, Lady Milthorpe began to exclaim about gowns and all that would be required, and Daniel, his tea now finished, rose to his feet and silently made his way from the room.

The conversation had gone well, he considered, but his own upset and shame remained, even though Isabella had attempted to encourage him to forget about such things and instead, to focus on what would come next – her marriage and removal to Lord Milthorpe's estate. He had let her down, he knew, and that guilt still drove itself firmly into his heart.

And how much do I now despise society?

A heavy cloud settled over his mind. Had it not been for society and their willingness to gossip and spread rumors, then Daniel would have had no concerns when he discovered Lord Newforth and Isabella. He would have been able to take Isabella back from his hand without concern and Lord Newforth would never have been able to make such a threat in the first place. Instead, Lord Newforth had spread out for Daniel what would happen to Isabella, if he did not receive what he desired – namely, Isabella as his wife – and he had used the judgment of society as his leverage.

I despise them all.

Gritting his teeth, Daniel made his way into his study and, after going to pour himself a small whisky, went to sit down at his desk. A bundle of letters and invitations sat waiting for him, ready for him to respond to, but he did not even reach for the first of the letters. Instead, he sat, stony-faced, as though the letters themselves were to blame. For the very first time, he realized just how much society had aided Lord Newforth in his dark deceptions, how much they had given him in his attempts to secure Isabella's hand. Had Lord Milthorpe not stepped in, had he not offered his hand willingly to Isabella, then Daniel did not know what sort of situation they might now have found themselves in. Either Isabella would have been facing the judgment of society, or she would have been betrothed to Lord Newforth!

"How much I owe him."

Muttering to himself, Daniel rubbed one hand over his eyes, feeling them tired and heavy. The situation had come out as best as it could have done, and yet, Daniel was still all too aware of his failings. At the same time, a slow-growing hatred of society and all that it supposedly offered began to take hold of him and he started to scowl, a fury growing in his heart all over again.

I do not want to be a part of the ton *any longer. I do not want to be a part of those who live for gossip and whispers, and who can so easily tear another person's life apart.* Letting out a sigh, he shook his head. *I will remain until Isabella's marriage is complete and, thereafter, I intend to make my way from London and return home, never again to come back to another London Season.*

CHAPTER FOUR

"Well?"

Patience laughed as Eleanor's eyebrow lifted gently.

"Yes, my dear cousin? What is it that you are asking me?"

"Your drawing!" Eleanor grinned as Patience rolled her eyes. "You did not think that I would forget about it, did you?"

"I hoped that you might," Patience laughed, pulling herself out of her chair and, thereafter, making her way across the drawing room. "Though you have always been quite determined, have you not?"

Eleanor shrugged.

"When I know what it is that I want, then yes, I will admit that I am so. And what I want at this moment is to see your beautiful drawings."

Rather touched by her friend's considerations of her, Patience found the drawing and, thereafter, walked across the room to hand it to her cousin.

"There, now. You cannot complain any longer."

This made Eleanor laugh aloud again, though that sound quickly died away when she took in the picture that Patience had drawn of the gentleman and the lady standing very close together, each looking into each other's eyes. She tilted her head one way, then the other, before letting out a small sigh, though Patience found herself rather anxious, worried about what her cousin would have to say.

"That is quite beautiful, Patience. I so admire your ability to capture such a moment."

Patience let out a breath of relief before smiling at her cousin.

"I am glad that you think well of it."

"Oh, more than that! I think it quite wonderful, truly! You have made Miss Spearton and Lord Milthorpe's fervent look stand out beautifully."

"I thank you." Reaching to pour the tea, Patience smiled at her cousin. "Tell me, have you had any gentleman callers of late?"

Eleanor giggled, the color heightening in her cheeks and giving her away.

"I might well have done."

"And might you tell me their names?"

"I might." Eleanor laughed as Patience rolled her eyes. "I will confess that there are some gentlemen that I think very well of indeed, but some that are less welcome to call upon me. Alas, the ones that came to call on me the most recently are the ones whom I am *less* inclined towards, though one I might consider."

"And what is his name?" Patience asked, only for the door to open and her mother to step in, closely followed by Christina and another lady, whom Patience did not recognize. Quickly she and Eleanor rose to their feet.

"Good afternoon, Patience, Eleanor. Forgive me for the

intrusion." Lady Osterley gestured to the as yet unintroduced lady, who appeared to be a little younger than their mother, but older than Patience herself. "Might I introduce Lady Tolerton?"

Patience dropped into a curtsey.

"Good afternoon, Lady Tolerton. It is very nice to make your acquaintance."

"And I yours." The lady had a warm, rich voice and a bright expression which made Patience smile. "I have known your mother for many years, though it has been some time since we have been in company together. I am delighted now to meet you, and especially to spend time with her again."

"How very nice," Christina murmured, coming to sit down. "I have rung the bell, Mama, so we shall soon have more tea."

"That will be lovely, I am sure."

Lady Tolerton made to sit down, only to pause as she looked at something on the table. A little unsure about what the lady was looking at, Patience tried not to appear rude, only for her eyes to flare as she saw the lady looking at the drawing she had done of Lord Milthorpe and Miss Spearton.

Her face flushed hot.

"Oh, do excuse me," she said, reaching for it. "I was only just–"

"Might you permit me to see it?" Lady Tolerton's eyebrows were lifted but her smile was still present. "I must say, it caught my interest because it is such a remarkable piece!"

There was very little for Patience to do but to agree, picking up her drawing and, with concern growing in her heart over what the lady might say, handing it to her. She watched Lady Tolerton's face as she studied the drawing, though, of course, Patience's mother was beaming with evident delight over how Patience's work was being so considered. Christina went to open the door for the tea tray and still, Patience stood quietly, still a little anxious about what was soon to be said about her work.

"My goodness." Lady Tolerton looked up from her scrutiny and, thereafter, shook her head in Patience's direction. "I do not think that I have ever seen work like this before!"

Still a little unsure of whether or not this was meant as a compliment, Patience glanced at her mother, who quickly smiled reassuringly.

"I – I thank you," she said, carefully, as Lady Tolerton looked up from the drawing, then shook her head.

"Goodness, it is quite remarkable how you have captured the look shared between two people," she continued, as a warm glow of pleasure began to build in Patience's chest. "Do you draw often?"

"She does, very often." Christina, who now began to serve the tea, threw a smile towards Patience. "But she does not show her work to anyone, which I think is a great pity!"

Lady Tolerton nodded fervently.

"I would quite agree! More people should see such talent. Have you ever thought about how you might go about sharing your art with others?"

Patience shook her head, taking her teacup from Christina.

"That has never been something I have considered, truth be told. I do enjoy my artwork, and finding new subjects to draw, but I have never once thought about doing anything with my drawings."

"Would you like to see some more?" Lady Osterley made her way directly across the room, without so much as glancing at Patience. "She has a lot of drawings and sketches here in the escritoire, though often even I am not allowed to see them!"

"But why is that?" Lady Tolerton exclaimed, looking at Patience with wide eyes. "You have such a talent, Lady Patience! Your work is remarkable, and I must say, I think even the *ton* should see such beauty!"

Patience flushed at the thought.

"There is not always great beauty in what I have drawn, Lady Tolerton. The last piece I drew was, in fact, something of a rarity for me. There are often times when I will exaggerate a person's features or the like, and I am not certain that everyone would appreciate my focus in that way."

Her fingers knitted together, her eyes darting this way and that as she looked from Christina to her mother and then back again, seeing how Lady Tolerton's eyes widened as she looked through Patience's pieces. Her mother was saying something, perhaps trying to describe what Patience had done in each piece, but Patience could not quite hear. Christina smiled encouragingly, but Patience felt herself growing tense all the same. It was the first time that someone else had seen her work in some time, and Patience prayed that Lady Tolerton would appreciate these just as much as she had the other.

An exclamation followed by a laugh made Patience's eyebrows lift high. Much to her surprise, Lady Tolerton was grinning broadly, holding a piece of artwork in her hand. Turning her head, she came over to Patience, gesturing to it.

"This is remarkable! It is Lord Westerlake, is it not?"

It took Patience a moment to answer, looking at the artwork and then up into the lady's face.

"Why, yes, it is."

"I knew it!" Lady Tolerton giggled, her eyes dancing.

"You have exaggerated the way he lifts his chin in that superior manner, as well as pressing out his nose a little more than it truly does."

Patience nodded, hoping that the lady would not think poorly of her for doing so.

"Yes, that is quite so."

"Remarkable. *Remarkable.*" Lady Tolerton said the same word twice but emphasized the second time a good deal more than the first, looking straight into Patience's eyes as though she wanted her to understand just how fervently she believed it. "I have not seen work like yours before and I think that you ought to find a way to share it with others."

Patience's eyebrows lifted.

"Do you not think that there might be some who would find what I have done a little... insulting?"

Lady Tolerton chuckled as she made her way back to the writing desk, setting the piece of artwork down.

"Does it matter if they do? I think that there will be far more members of the *ton* thinking very highly of your work and, mayhap, they too might soon desire themselves to be drawn in such a fashion." She smiled. "In fact, I know that The London Chronicle has been looking for something new and interesting to include in its publication. If I could be so bold, might I suggest that I ask if they would print your work there?"

Patience blinked rapidly, the question catching her by surprise. It was one thing to talk about what it might be like to share her work with other members of society, but quite another to suggest having it printed in a newspaper!

"Oh, that would certainly single you out, would it not?" Lady Osterley clapped her hands rather than looking at all concerned. "You would become well known in society, and there might be many a gentleman who would think it quite wonderful to have a young lady such as yourself on his arm!"

Patience shook her head.

"Mama, by the very same thought, there might be many a gentleman who would not come near me because of such a thing! They might desire a young lady who would do nothing other than smile and do just as she ought, without having even the least bit of interest about her."

Christina reached out and touched Patience's hand.

"But would you like such a thing as that, Patience? Would you truly be contented with a husband who would not even *know* of your desire to draw and paint? Would you be happy, married to someone who tried to quash that desire within you, rather than encourage it?"

Patience opened her mouth to say that she did not see any difficulty in that, only to snap her mouth closed again. The truth was, she did not want to marry someone who would not be in the least bit interested in what *her* passion was. With a small sigh, she turned her gaze away from her sister and looked down at her teacup.

"Might you permit me to see if your drawing of this lovely couple could be printed in The London Chronicle?" Lady Tolerton asked, gently. "I do not mean to put you under any sort of pressure, but I do believe that your work would be appreciated by many."

Uncertain as to what she wanted to do, Patience looked from her mother to Christina, and then back to Lady Tolerton. Every face had an encouraging smile on it, and Patience let out a slow breath, closing her eyes for a moment.

"Might it be possible to have it published anonymously?"

"Anonymously?" her mother interrupted before Lady

Tolerton could reply. "Why would you wish to do such a thing?"

"Because that way, I will be able to ascertain the reaction of the *ton* before deciding whether or not I ought to publish more – and whether I ought to put my name to them also!" Patience smiled as her mother's lips puckered. "I know that you believe that there will be a great deal of happiness and delight in what I have drawn, but I should like to see that for myself, first."

"A wise consideration," Lady Tolerton agreed, smiling at Patience. "I think it a good suggestion. Thank you, Lady Patience. I know that we have only just become acquainted, and yet here you are, trusting that I shall do just as I have said, and print your work in The London Chronicle!" Her eyes shone with expectant hope. "I am quite certain that you will see a good deal of delight in all that you have done here, Lady Patience. And that, I hope, will encourage you even more."

"I hope so." There was a writhing in her stomach that told Patience that she was still anxious about agreeing to this and it grew all the more as she watched Lady Tolerton pick up her drawing of Miss Spearton and Lord Milthorpe. "I saw that moment at the announcement of Lord Milthorpe and Miss Spearton's betrothal," she said, as Lady Tolerton nodded. "I kept it in my mind until I was able to put pencil to paper. I do not mind in the least if The London Chronicle names them since it is a piece without any exaggeration – but for others, I may wish their identities to be kept a secret."

"Though some will identify them regardless," Christina put in, quietly, as their mother nodded. "Your work is better than you realize, Patience."

"Mayhap."

Wishing now to change the subject, Patience took a breath and, with a smile, asked Lady Tolerton about any recent events that she had attended. Much to her joy, the lady was more than willing to speak, and soon, the conversation had changed entirely, from Patience's artwork to something completely different. However, at the back of her mind, Patience could not forget what was going to happen to her artwork, silently hoping that all would be just as her mother and Lady Tolerton had said.

CHAPTER FIVE

"Have you seen this?"
Daniel started in surprise as the door to the dining room was practically flung open, causing his coffee to slosh around in his cup.

"Good gracious, Isabella, whatever is the matter that you must surprise me in this manner?"

"I am in The London Chronicle!"

All at once, Daniel's stomach lurched furiously and he set his coffee cup down in an instant, his eyes rounding. To be in The London Chronicle was no good thing, for that surely must mean that it was nothing but gossip! Rising to his feet, he grasped Isabella's hand as she set down The London Chronicle on the table before him.

"You must not be concerned. Whatever has been said, it will be dealt with as quickly as can be."

Isabella blinked at him, confusion in her eyes.

"Whatever do you mean?"

"Something must have been written about you, yes?" he asked, gesturing to the paper. "That is why you have rushed through to tell me about it?"

Much to his surprise, Isabella laughed and then shook her head.

"No, no, not in the least! I have not been written about and I am in no way concerned about it, I assure you."

A frown pulled at Daniel's forehead.

"Then what is it?"

"It is this!" Turning, Isabella pulled the paper open and then showed it to him. It took Daniel a few moments to understand what it meant but, after understanding hit him, he caught his breath, his eyebrows lifting. "It is beautiful, is it not?"

"I am surprised at it, I must say." Daniel picked up the newspaper for a closer look, turning his head just a little as he took in the picture that had been drawn of Isabella and Lord Milthorpe. "Someone must have drawn this the night of the ball, though I did not see any artists present." He looked at the picture again, trying to find a name. "It does not say who has drawn this."

"No, it does not, though I now think to write to The London Chronicle and discover it."

Daniel smiled at his sister, seeing the light in her eyes and hearing the happiness in her voice.

"It sounds as though you are delighted with it, my dear."

"I am."

"Even though it expresses an affection that is not truly there between yourself and Lord Milthorpe?" The smile on Isabella's face flickered and instantly, Daniel realized he had unintentionally upset her. "Forgive me, I did not mean to–"

"It is something to aspire to, is it not?" Her voice had softened, and Daniel dropped his head, a little embarrassed that he had spoken without thinking. "Something that I hope will soon exist between myself and Lord Milthorpe.

This drawing is a beautiful picture of what I desire, of what I long for. I cannot think of anything better than that."

"Then I am glad for you that the artist has chosen to print this artwork in The London Chronicle. And," he continued, pulling Isabella close and dropping a kiss to the top of her head, "it will make Lord Newforth all the angrier, for the *ton* will now believe that you are quite in love with Lord Milthorpe and he with you, and what could be more wonderful than that?"

"Indeed." Isabella sighed, smiled, and then looked up at him. "Though you do not appear to be in the least bit contented at present." Her smile began to fade away, as she searched his face with her gaze. "I do not want you to be upset any longer, brother. The match is made, I shall be contented and all will be well."

Daniel tried to smile in return, but his expression seemed stuck, a little too fixed.

"I am glad in that regard, but I must say that I struggle a great deal with the pressure that society has brought to bear. Had they not been inclined towards gossip, had Lord Newforth not been able to use them as a threat, then you might now be free and able to make your own decision as regards your future."

Isabella lifted her shoulders and then let them fall, a small sigh on her lips.

"Alas, what can be done? It is not as though we can turn from society, not as though we can force them to do what we wish them to do, is it?"

"No, I suppose we cannot. But it does mean that I can decide not to be a part of it any longer."

His sister's eyebrows lifted.

"What do you mean?"

"It means simply that." Daniel sat back down and

picked up his coffee. "I will do what I must this Season but, once you are wed, I have no intention of returning to London again. Nor will I be as invested in it as I was before, for you have suffered greatly because of the *ton*. Lord Newforth used them to his advantage, and that means that I no longer wish to be as involved with society as before. I used to think that it was a wonderful thing to be in the *ton*, to be an esteemed member of society. Now, however, I see it quite clearly. It is a monster, ready to devour anyone it pleases at the smallest whim."

Isabella sat down beside him, reaching for the teapot.

"I can understand your concerns, but I do not think that there is a great need to be so pulled away from it all."

"*I* do," Daniel answered, firmly. "I shall do what I must for the time being, but thereafter, I will no longer be as present as I have been before." His sister flattened her lips as though she wanted to say something more, but had chosen not to, seeing that he was more than a little determined about what he wanted to do. "But I am happy that you appear to be a good deal more contented with Lord Milthorpe than I had expected." Daniel smiled briefly, then finished his coffee. "Now, I must go and finish the invitations for your betrothal ball. I do hope that you are looking forward to it?"

Isabella nodded.

"Very much."

"That is good."

"And you will still attend the soiree this evening, will you not?"

With a small smile, Daniel rose to his feet.

"I shall, of course. Just because I seek to step back from society does not mean that I will no longer attend all that we have been invited to."

"I am glad, for I do not think that I can face society without you as yet," Isabella answered, her eyes becoming a little damp. "I am still afraid that Lord Newforth will do something, although I have become betrothed."

Daniel shook his head.

"You need not fear him, I assure you. I have not seen him since the moment that you announced your betrothal, and I must hope that he has now left society, given that he has lost the battle for what he desired."

"I hope so." Isabella took a breath and then picked up her tea. "Until this evening, then, Hastings."

"MILTHORPE." Daniel shook his friend's hand, glancing around the room. "A busy soiree, it seems."

"It is." Lord Milthorpe leaned into Daniel's space a little more. "Lord Newforth is present also, I am afraid."

Fire roared up Daniel's chest.

"Lord Newforth?"

"Yes."

Daniel closed his eyes.

"I told Isabella that I had not seen him since the announcement of her betrothal and hoped that he had stepped away from society altogether."

Lord Milthorpe set his jaw.

"It seems that he is determined to linger in society, my friend. Though I am sure that he can do nothing to you or Isabella, not now." He scowled. "Though he has not come to speak with me, I have caught the many dark glances he has thrown in my direction."

"It would be best to ignore him," Daniel stated, firmly. "He seeks to intimidate, mayhap. But he shall not be successful. I will have to warn Isabella so that she is not surprised."

"I will tell her." Lord Milthorpe lifted his chin a little, a darkness in his eyes. "I will not permit Lord Newforth to upset her. He has done enough of that already, and it angers me a great deal that nothing of consequence has happened to him, given his dreadful behavior."

A little surprised, although rather pleased that his friend had expressed himself so firmly over Isabella and his concern for her, Daniel moved so that his back was to the wall, and looked out amongst the crowd. The room was full of guests, though Lord Benford had at least four rooms open for all of his guests to make their way through. At some point, Daniel intended to go to the card room although he hoped that Lord Newforth would not be there also.

"I think that I will go in search of her now, if I might?" Lord Milthorpe put one hand on Daniel's shoulder for a moment. "She is with your mother, I expect?"

Daniel nodded.

"Yes, she is. Though my mother is quite delighted with that drawing which appeared in The London Chronicle, so be warned that she will, no doubt, speak to you of that and nothing else."

Lord Milthorpe chuckled quietly.

"Truth be told, I thought that drawing quite wonderful and am also truly delighted with it." His smile grew just a little. "I think that the look shared between us speaks of what I hope my marriage to Isabella will be, and in that, I will be glad to speak with anyone about it, including Lady Hastings."

With another smile and a nod, Milthorpe stepped away and left Daniel to stand alone. Folding his arms over his chest, he continued to search the room for any sign of Lord

Newforth, wondering what dark intentions the gentleman might have planned. Did he think to say something to upset Daniel or Isabella? Surely, as Lord Milthorpe had said, there was nothing that he could say to do such a thing? It was not as though he could announce that he had tried to force Daniel's hand, that he had pulled Isabella unwillingly into his arms? Thinking about the drawing in The London Chronicle, Daniel felt a sense of relief pour into him which then molded into gratitude for the artist. Whether they realized it or not, they had helped to convince the *ton* of the strength of Isabella's and Lord Milthorpe's connection, and that could only be a good thing.

I am not going to ruminate over what Lord Newforth might or might not do, he told himself, firmly. *I cannot. It is a waste of my time, when there are a good many other things I can put my mind to.*

Out of the corner of his eye, he caught sight of someone studying him.

Turning his head fully, he took in a young lady who, like him, was standing to the back of the room and was studying him with a careful eye, though, once she saw him looking at her, she turned her head away in an instant, her cheeks flushing hot.

Daniel frowned. The young lady was now a little embarrassed, given that he had seen her watching him. Her cheeks were a little flushed, her fair hair was pulled back into intricate braids with only a few small curls at her temples and her ears. She caught one lip with the other, biting it gently and Daniel could not help but smile, feeling the need now to put her at ease.

"You are standing alone, much as I am doing." He lifted one eyebrow just a little, though made no move to step closer to her. "Do you not enjoy a soiree?"

She glanced at him, then turned her gaze away again.

"It is not that I do not enjoy it, sir, but rather that I am waiting for my mother and sister to finish a conversation that I was not a part of. I do not want to interrupt them so, thus, you find me here."

Turning to face her, Daniel offered her a small smile.

"Do you not have any other acquaintances here, my Lady?"

"I have some. But for my own reasons, I am standing alone for a time."

A little intrigued by this, Daniel studied her again, but said nothing, watching her carefully and wondering what it was that she might have meant. The lady's cheeks were still flushed, but her eyes darted from one side of the room to the other, as though she was searching for something or someone, much as he was doing.

"Will you not tell me what your reasons are?" It was a little rude of him to ask her such a thing, but the conversation, as a whole, was already improper, given that they had not been introduced. Daniel's eyebrows lifted all the higher, but the lady only shook her head, offering him only a very small and brief smile in response. "The Viscount Hastings." He inclined his head, though it was not a complete nor proper bow. "I understand that this is no formal introduction, though it shall have to do, for the nonce."

The lady's cheeks flushed all the more.

"Lady Patience. My father is the Earl of Osterley though he is not going about in society at present."

"I see." Daniel studied her again, taking her in fully. She was, he considered, quite beautiful if not, mayhap, a little reserved. "You will not tell me of your reasons for staying away from your other acquaintances here, then?"

She shrugged.

"I see no need to, though you may tell me of *your* purposes in standing alone if you wish it."

At this, Daniel chuckled, a sense of happiness beginning to slip into him.

"I am afraid that I have no purposes, Lady Patience. All I have is a desire to stand alone and to study those present for a time."

"For what reason is that?"

Daniel shook his head, unwilling to tell her anything about his present concerns over society.

"It is simply because I am a little fatigued, that is all."

"I understand." She spoke in such a way that Daniel could hear the slight inflection in her voice which, to his mind, spoke of a lack of belief. He railed at it internally, only to remind himself that such a thing did not matter, given that they were both perfect strangers and, therefore, did not need to have even the smallest level of trust between them. She glanced at him, a question in her eyes, though it took her another few moments to speak it. Daniel waited in silence. "Might I ask if your sister is Miss Spearton?"

"Yes, she is." A little surprised at the lady's connection to his sister, Daniel frowned. "Are you acquainted?"

The lady shook her head.

"No, we are not. I have recently heard of her betrothal and thus, that is how I know of her connection to you."

"I see."

Again, the lady's green eyes met his and then pulled away again.

"Her betrothal must have been a great delight to you. Lord Milthorpe is, I understand, a close friend of yours."

The frown on Daniel's forehead only deepened. This, he reminded himself, was the very reason he was trying to pull away from the *ton*. He had no desire whatsoever to have anything to do with society any longer, but yet, it was presenting itself to him all the same. The only reason that Lady Patience knew of his connection to Isabella was because there would have been those in the *ton* who would have told her of it. He did not know if there had been any particular attitude to that conversation, whether or not there would have been those who would have spoken well of them, or spoken ill. He had to pray that it was kind and generous remarks which had been made of them, but he could not be sure of it.

"It will be a good marriage," was all he said, choosing not to make any further remarks. "Now, if you will excuse me, Lady Patience, I think I shall attempt to be sociable again."

Stepping away from her, he felt her gaze linger on him still, and his skin prickled uncomfortably. He did not want her studying him, did not like to be the subject of her perusal. The last thing he wanted was whispers spread from one person to another within the *ton*.

"Good evening, Lord Hastings."

Daniel scowled, coming to an abrupt stop as he came face to face with the very person he had been trying to spy out to avoid him.

"Lord Newforth. I have nothing to say to you."

"Oh, but I have much to say to you." Lord Newforth took a step closer, and Daniel retreated back to where he had come from – not from fear, but from a desire to make certain that very few people could overhear whatever Lord Newforth was going to insist upon saying. "Come now, Lord Hastings! You are not afraid of me, are you?"

Daniel drew himself up as tall as he could.

"Not in the least," he grated, irritated by the gentleman's suggestion. "I have no wish to talk to you, Newforth. I presume that much is clear but yet, it seems, you are going to disregard what *I* desire and instead, force yourself upon me."

"Much as I did your sister."

Those words, as well as the cold, dark smile that glittered across Lord Newforth's face made Daniel's stomach twist, sending fire through him as he fought to keep his composure. Was that what Lord Newforth wanted? Did he hope that Daniel would embarrass himself in front of the *ton,* so that he might then spread rumors and whispers about him to shame him all the more? It was quite clear to Daniel that the man wanted some sort of revenge and this, it seemed, was his way of going about it.

Swallowing hard, Daniel let his hands curl into tight fists but otherwise, said nothing.

"You think that you have bested me, do you not?" Lord Newforth hissed, coming even closer to Daniel, his eyes narrowed and like shards of glass, ready to push into Daniel's skin. "You think that you have succeeded by marrying your sister to your best friend?"

"I do not think that I have," Daniel retorted, forcing himself to keep his voice low, "I *know* that I have done so. It was clear to me from the beginning what it was that you desired when it came to my sister – but you shall not have her, Newforth."

Lord Newforth's expression grew ugly.

"You know nothing about me."

"On the contrary," Daniel answered, his lip curling. "I know that you are without fortune, that you have frittered what you had away on gambling and on visiting houses of disrepute, and no doubt, that these are still difficulties for you. You did not desire my sister out of any attraction to her, out of any sincere desire to take her as your wife, but solely because of your interest in her fortune. *That* is what drove you to her, *that* is what pulled at you over and over again. I may not have the highest title within society, but I do have an excellent fortune and Isabella, therefore, an increased dowry. With that, she will also be given a yearly income from my estate, as was pledged in my father's will. Knowing this, it is *that* which you sought rather than anything else, Lord Newforth, and it is because of that situation that I refused you my sister's hand. I am *glad* that she is to wed Lord Milthorpe, and all the more impressed with his consideration and care for her, for it is that which has driven him to offer for her hand. I think that they will have a very happy and successful marriage, and I am all the more delighted that *you* have lost what you once desired. There is nothing you can do that will take her from him."

Lord Newforth's jaw set tight, his face turning a shade of red that Daniel had rarely seen on a person's face before. Daniel, however, held the gentleman's gaze, almost daring him to speak again, to find something more to say.

"You may have succeeded there," Lord Newforth eventually whispered, "but I will make certain that your own success in matrimony fails utterly, Hastings."

At this, Daniel let out a short, sharp laugh, making Lord Newforth's eyes round.

"You are mistaken if you think that I have any interest in matrimony," he replied, anger in his tone now. "Or any interest in society, in fact. You have failed, Lord Newforth, and you shall fail again."

At this, Lord Newforth reared back, looking as though he wanted to strike Daniel hard across the face, his other hand reaching out to grab Daniel's arm, holding him in place. Daniel snatched a breath, blood pounding in his ears, afraid now of what fury might drive Lord Newforth to do.

"Ah, Lord Hastings."

A calm, clear voice interrupted them, and Lord Newforth instantly dropped Daniel's arm and stepped back, though his breathing was ragged now.

"I have quite lost my mother and sister." Lady Patience smiled at Daniel, her expression a stark contrast to the fury and panic that had been spreading through Daniel's chest. "Might I beg of you to walk with me until I find them again? I think standing alone at the back of the drawing room is something of a mistake, for I have found myself quite bored and lacking any fine conversation!"

Daniel cleared his throat, feeling a little lost as he looked into Lady Patience's eyes, trying to find a sense of equilibrium again.

"I – why yes, of course."

"I thank you." She smiled still and then turned her attention to Lord Newforth. "My sincere apologies to you for the interruption, good sir. Good evening."

Daniel had no other choice but to walk away from Lord Newforth, his blood still running hot in his veins as he made his way through the drawing room with Lady Patience on his arm. He did not know what to say, wondering if he owed her some sort of explanation, only to shake his head to himself.

"You must think that a very strange situation to have witnessed," he muttered, not quite sure what else to say. Should he be grateful that she had interrupted in such a way? That she had prevented Lord Newforth from doing whatever it was that he had intended? He did not know.

"I did not hear anything, if that is what you are asking me," came the reply, "though I will admit to seeing anger on both your face and on the other gentleman's face."

"Lord Newforth."

There came no flash of recognition into her green eyes.

"I am not acquainted with him." She smiled sadly. "I mayhap ought not to have interrupted in the way that I did, Lord Hastings, but I was concerned that Lord Newforth was about to do something quite terrible and, knowing that your sister is, at this moment, filled with happiness at her betrothal, I could not imagine what Lord Newforth's action might do."

Daniel frowned.

"Are you acquainted with my sister?"

Lady Patience shook her head.

"No, I am not. Though I am well aware that her betrothal has only been announced very recently and, since there is the drawing in The London Chronicle too, then it is well known to all of London society just how happy she must be at this moment."

Softening, Daniel smiled, his heart beginning to steady itself now that he was away from Lord Newforth.

"It is surprising that you would care so much for a young lady who is not even someone acquainted with you."

"Is it?" Lady Patience tilted her head. "I do not think so, I confess. I assume that any young lady would show care and consideration for others, knowing that we are all in the same position here in London."

"Position?"

A slight smile touched the edges of her mouth, her eyes brighter now.

"We are here to wed, just as your sister's purpose was," she said, making Daniel flush with a sudden embarrassment. He ought to have understood what she meant. "I am glad that she has found happiness with Lord Milthorpe. That is why I interrupted your conversation with Lord Newforth's, though I hope that I did not do wrong."

"No, no, not in the least," Daniel assured her, quickly. "You are very kind to have done such a thing, Lady Patience. Most considerate of you, assuredly."

Her eyes smiled up into his and for a moment, Daniel's heart swelled with something other than relief over being taken from the anger of Lord Newforth. Then, it was gone, fading just as quickly as it had come, as he turned his head away.

"Ah, Patience, there you are."

"Here I am, Mama." Lady Patience released his arm and then, after a quick smile at him, stepped towards her mother, leaving Daniel behind. There was no requirement, no expectation for him to step forward and introduce himself, he realized, and for that, he was grateful. Suddenly, the only thing that he wanted to do was find Isabella and make certain that she was safe. With Lord Newforth present and in such an angry frame of mind, Daniel *had* to stay close to Isabella. It was the only way that she could be protected though, he feared, the threat would not dissipate for some time, mayhap only after Isabella was wed and he was far away from society.

Though I have seen that not everyone in society is as cruel, nor as eager to gossip as others, he thought to himself, casting a quick glance over his shoulder. Lady Patience was laughing at something that someone had said, and that bright, joyful moment made him smile. Despite Lord Newforth's threat, it was clear to Daniel that Lady Patience, at least, was quite determined to protect Isabella, someone she had not even been introduced to! That was a kindness indeed and, for just a moment, it made Daniel feel a little better about society.

Though it was only for a moment.

CHAPTER SIX

*P*atience smiled to herself as she set her pencil down, taking in the figure she had just drawn. It was just as she had seen him the previous evening, standing stalwart at the side of the drawing-room, his arms loose by his sides but his head held high, his eyes sharp and filled with an uncertainty that she had been able almost to sense from him.

The soiree had been enjoyable, of course, but Patience had found herself a little overwhelmed by the crush of bodies. To her mind, there had been too many guests for one townhouse and thus, she had stepped away for a few minutes, promising her mother that she would remain in sight of her and Christina. Christina had not suffered any of the difficulties nor the struggle that Patience had, seeming to relish being in the crowd of guests. Patience had smiled to herself, watching the way that Christina had laughed and smiled and conversed with various gentlemen and ladies, thinking to herself just how very different they were in their personalities... and it was then that she had seen him. Lord Hastings, as she now knew him to be, had made his way across the room to speak directly with Lord Milthorpe, whom Patience knew by sight rather than because they had been introduced. She had tried not to look, as the two gentlemen had conversed, hearing the two low voices and, to her mind, a note of concern in both.

When Lord Milthorpe had stepped away, Patience had expected Lord Hastings to do the same, but he had not. Instead, he had stayed precisely where he was, moving back just a fraction so that he stood with his back to the wall, looking out at everyone in the drawing room, just as she was. She had been uncertain whether or not he had known of her presence and, though she knew very well that she ought not to turn her head and look at him, something about his presence had encouraged her to do that very thing. The image had fixed itself in her mind and Patience had known at once that this was a gentleman she would *have* to draw, someone she would have to capture on paper. A brooding figure, mayhap, she had thought, tilting her head to take in his features a little better.

And then, he had turned his head.

A sudden flush of heat rushed through her as she recalled the moment he had turned to look at her, clearly aware that she had been studying him. It had been an awkward moment, one where she had felt herself more than a little embarrassed and yet, at the same time, feeling a flickering sense of interest in him. It was not something she had ever expected to feel and yet, it was there nonetheless, beckoning her closer. Part of her had expected him to roll his eyes and look away, or to turn his head away again and pretend that nothing of note had taken place but, instead, he had begun to speak. Their conversation had been brief, and Patience had been careful not to say anything that might be in the least bit encouraging, aware that they had not been introduced. But then, he had introduced himself and she had done the same. It had been a pleasure to know his title, to recognize who he was, in relation to Miss Spearton and to Lord Milthorpe also, though she had not said very much in that regard. He had chosen to step away from her, excusing himself in a genial manner, only for another gentleman to step into his path.

That was most confusing.

It was not in her nature to be forward, to push herself into conversations and situations where she had no right to be. She had not been able to make out any of the two gentlemen's conversation, but she had been able to *see* the fury that had been building between them. It had been clear to her that Lord Hastings was doing his level best to stay as calm as he could, though she had seen the way that his hands had tightened into fists as he spoke – but Lord Newforth had been quite different. There had been anger in every single movement of his frame, from the way that he had filled the space between himself and Lord Hastings, to the tightness of his frame. When he had pulled back just a little, reaching out to grab Lord Hastings' arm, Patience had found herself reacting without having ever intended to do anything at all.

"Though I am still glad that I did such a thing."

"You are speaking to yourself now, Patience?"

Whirling around, Patience put one hand to her heart.

"Goodness, Eleanor, I did not hear you step into the room!"

"I did call your name thrice," Eleanor teased, though there was a twinkle in her eye that made Patience question whether such a thing was true or not. "What is it that you are doing?"

"Drawing." Patience held out her sketch of Lord Hastings to her cousin, knowing that she would be determined to look at it, even if Patience had tried her best to hide it from her. "It was from the soiree yesterday."

Eleanor's eyes widened.

"This is Lord Hastings, is it not?"

"It is."

Eleanor beamed at her.

"And are you going to send it to The London Chronicle? I saw your drawing of Lord Milthorpe and Miss Spearton and thought it quite wonderful! I have been telling everyone that it was your work."

Something seemed to shrivel inside Patience.

"You have been telling the *ton* that it was I who drew it?"

Her cousin nodded, still smiling.

"Of course I have! Why would I not?"

A low groan escaped Patience as she covered her face with both of her hands.

"Oh, Eleanor, I wish you had spoken to me first! I was not certain that I *wanted* people to know that I was the artist!"

"Why ever not?"

Patience threw up her hands.

"Because I do not know what they will think of me! I am here to find a match, am I not? What if the gentlemen of London think it dreadful that a lady should have her work published in The London Chronicle?"

Eleanor only sniffed.

"If there was such a complaint, then I would think those gentlemen were only jealous of your ability. After all, there is nothing wrong with a lady drawing and painting, is there? It is one of the things that gentlemen of the *ton* hope that we will excel in!"

"I suppose it is, yes." Patience laughed and then shook her head. "You are quite incorrigible, Eleanor. No matter what kind of obstacle or concern I attempt to throw up, you always have an answer."

Her cousin chuckled.

"I thank you. So you will have it published, then?"

"This one?"

Eleanor nodded.

"Yes, that one. I think it is quite magnificent, and I am sure many in the *ton* will think well of it."

Still uncertain, Patience looked at her drawing again. There was something that held her back inwardly, though she could not say what it was. It could not be that she wanted Lord Hastings' approval, surely? She did not even know the gentleman very well and yet, all the same, she felt herself uncertain as to whether or not she wanted to share this with the *ton*.

"You cannot think to hold this back, surely?" Eleanor smiled at her, questions in her eyes. "It will be well thought of, I am sure."

Patience sighed and then shrugged lightly.

"I suppose I can have no reason to refuse, then. Lady Tolerton – the one who first published my drawing in The London Chronicle – has already written to me stating that they are now requesting another drawing to put into it and thus, I suppose I can send her this one."

"Excellent!" Eleanor clapped her hands and then beamed at Patience. "I shall wait until you have sent it and thereafter, we can take our walk through the park."

With a quick roll of her eyes, Patience looked at her cousin and then spoke with a mock weariness in her voice.

"You are going to insist that I do so, are you not? You will not let me wait to send it until I return?"

Eleanor grinned, her eyes dancing.

"Of course I must insist. How else can I be sure that you will do it?"

With a laugh, Patience promised that she would do so just as quickly as she could and, still with a lingering trepidation, set to preparing her drawing.

∽

"I DO NOT KNOW much about Lord Hastings." Eleanor glanced at Patience before returning her gaze to the path ahead of them. "Might I ask what made *him* your focus?"

Patience considered her answer.

"Truth be told, Eleanor, sometimes I only need to see someone for them to make a distinct impression upon me. It was strange, in a way, seeing him standing as he did, for the soiree was in full swing and yet, he came first to talk to Lord Milthorpe and, thereafter, to stand alone. He has a striking profile, and there was also a heaviness in his expression which caught my attention." Seeing Eleanor's eyebrows lift, Patience wondered whether she ought to tell her about what else had occurred and, after a moment, chose to do so. Eleanor's eyebrows lifted high as Patience spoke, her eyes rounding, but she did not interrupt even once, waiting until Patience had finished. "So I do not know what it was that upset Lord Newforth, nor Lord Hastings, in that manner, but I was glad that he was not angry with me for intervening as I did."

"Good gracious, it sounds as though Lord Newforth was attempting to intimidate Lord Hastings in some way, though I cannot imagine why he would do so! How very strange." Eleanor linked arms with Patience. "I have heard the *ton* say of late that Lord Hastings has begun to pull away from those in society, almost as though he does not wish to be known by any of them. It is somewhat strange, for the announcement of his sister's betrothal is meant to be a wonderful thing, is it not? The invitations for her betrothal ball are due to come out later this week and yet, Lord Hastings seems to be pulling back, pulling away from all of us. I cannot imagine what it is that troubles him, but it appears that he is quite determined to step back, as you witnessed at the soiree."

"I do not know." Rounding the corner of the path, Patience was met with a few gathered crowds of ladies and gentlemen, though the fashionable hour was still not quite begun. She began to walk more slowly, her gaze darting over each and every face, though she was not sure who it was she was looking for. "I do not claim even the smallest knowledge of Lord Hastings' character and–"

"If I might interrupt, I should tell you that Lord Hastings has the most excellent character."

A flush of heat rushed into Patience's cheeks as she turned her head to see a young lady looking at them, her chin tilted upwards, and a flash of fire in her eyes. She recognized her at once, though they had never been introduced.

"I ought not to interrupt your conversation, I know," the young lady continued, taking a step closer to Patience and Eleanor, "but if someone is to speak of my brother, then I will do all that I must to defend him."

"You quite mistake our intentions, Miss Spearton." Patience inclined her head by way of greeting. "It is not our intention to speak poorly about your brother. Rather, I was simply saying that I did not know anything about him as yet, given that we were only just introduced the previous evening... and that was not even a proper introduction! Please forgive us for upsetting you."

Miss Spearton's eyes flashed and, for whatever reason, she did not appear to believe Patience.

"I have heard a few of the whispers about my brother only this afternoon," she snapped, tossing her head. "I would not like it if there were others who intended to speak ill of him even more. You may say that your intentions were not to injure him but–"

"Ah, Lady Patience. Good afternoon."

Patience swallowed hard as she dipped into a curtsey, the warmth in her face intensifying.

"Lord Hastings."

Miss Spearton's gaze darted between Patience and the gentleman.

"You are acquainted with this lady, brother?"

"Of course I am. I would not have greeted her otherwise." Lord Hastings looked from his sister to Patience and then back again. "I do hope that there is nothing of concern here?"

Miss Spearton's eyes narrowed just a little.

"I overheard you mentioned in conversation and thought to come to your defense. I have heard the recent rumors about you, and I certainly do not wish anyone to add to them. Therefore, though it was a little rude I admit, I did interrupt to state quite the opposite of what *might* have been being said."

"Though it was not needed, I assure you," Eleanor put in as Patience nodded fervently. "We were not saying anything derogatory."

Lord Hastings, rather than smile and state that he quite understood, immediately scowled.

"But you were speaking of me, Lady Patience?"

A trifle unsettled at his response, Patience cleared her throat and then lifted her chin.

"You are mistaken if you believe that I am in any way inclined towards gossip or the like, Lord Hastings. My cousin was asking me about the soiree, and I told her of our less than perfect introduction to one another, that is all."

"I see." The scowl did not lift from his face. "Yes, it was not as it ought to have been, I suppose." His gaze then turned towards Eleanor, who only smiled at him. "And we have not been introduced as yet, I do not think."

Eleanor bobbed into a quick curtsey.

"Lord Hastings, I was just saying to my cousin that I did not know you *or* your character, so I am very glad to be able to make your acquaintance."

The defense that such words brought made Patience's heart skip a beat as she hid a smile. Eleanor had, in her own clear and distinct way, stated that she had not been saying anything untoward about Lord Hastings and, from the way that his lips flattened, Patience was quite sure that he understood precisely what it was she had meant by such words. It seemed, however, that he was not in the least bit pleased.

"How very good to make your acquaintance." His voice had dropped low, a slight darkness about his expression now. "I do hope that the impression I made upon you, Lady Patience, might have given you a slight indication as to the sort of gentleman I purport to be."

"Indeed, it did." Patience smiled warmly in the hope that this would bring an end to the conversation, that there would be nothing now to concern him. "Did you enjoy the soiree last evening, Lord Hastings?"

"No."

The short, sharp answer took Patience by surprise, and

her smile dropped from her face. Lord Hastings now appeared to be in something of a dark mood, not even smiling at them any longer. Could it be that he believed what his sister had suggested they had been doing, even though both herself and Eleanor had stated, quite clearly, that they had done nothing of the sort? After what Miss Spearton had mentioned about the rumors, mayhap he too had come to hear of them and was now concerned.

"You must forgive my brother." Miss Spearton, her bright expression appearing forced rather than in the least bit genuine, smiled tightly. "Last evening did bring something of a trial with it, but you cannot say that there was no true enjoyment, Hastings!"

Lord Hastings shrugged and turned his head away, making a flush of embarrassment rush through Patience.

"There may have been a moment or two of enjoyment – when I was in your company and Lord Milthorpe's also, Isabella – but I cannot say there was much if I am to be truthful."

Patience closed her eyes, the tension she had felt in their conversation thus far now changing into one of sheer mortification. She had thought that he might feel something akin to appreciation over what had taken place last evening, for that was what he had expressed, had it not been? She had not thought that he would speak so darkly about the soiree, as though even their brief conversation and the incident she had broken into thereafter had meant nothing. Her stomach twisted and she swallowed tightly, before opening her eyes and forcing a bright smile to her face.

"It has been a pleasure to see you again, Lord Hastings." She did not look at him directly, quickly moving her gaze to Miss Spearton. "And Miss Spearton, though we have not been formally introduced, it has also been my delight to speak with you. I do hope that you enjoy the fashionable hour. Do excuse us."

Eleanor sniffed, her chin lifting.

"A delight," she murmured, echoing Patience's words. "Good afternoon."

"Good afternoon," Miss Spearton answered, though Lord Hastings himself said nothing.

As Patience walked away, her face grew hot with embarrassment and a flicker of anger, frustrated that the gentleman had spoken in such an unkind manner.

"Goodness, Lord Hastings is either cruel, inconsiderate or unthinking!" Eleanor linked her arm through Patience's again, tugging her lightly. "You are quite all right, are you not?"

Patience blinked quickly and then turned her head away from Eleanor so that her cousin would not see the tears that had suddenly sprung into her eyes.

"I am quite well."

"You are upset."

Patience's shoulders dropped.

"A little. After what took place last evening, as I told you, I would have thought that Lord Hastings might have expressed appreciation, rather than stating how little he had enjoyed the evening. The way that he spoke was most unfair, and it made me feel deeply embarrassed."

"Which I think his sister felt also," Eleanor said, gently. "It is quite clear to me that she did not think well of what her brother said. After speaking of these rumors – which, no doubt, Lord Hastings is well aware of also – it seems to me that he does not care whether or not they are spoken about him or not! Though Miss Spearton is more than a little concerned."

"Yes, I could see that." Trying to push the conversation

from her mind, Patience bit her lip, suddenly now a little worried about the drawing that she had sent to The London Chronicle. What would Viscount Hastings think of her drawing? Would he be displeased? Or would he consider it innocuous, perhaps even be a little delighted that she had chosen him as her subject?

Her misgivings continued to grow as she made her way through the park, and Patience now began to wish that she had not agreed to send that drawing into the newspaper.

But now, it was much too late.

CHAPTER SEVEN

*D*aniel cleared his throat, clasped his hands behind his back, and looked his friend straight in the eye.

"I do not know what it is that you mean."

"I think you do." Lord Milthorpe's gaze sharpened. "You have been pulling back from society, standing with a somewhat unpleasant look on your face at most events, and I am sure that you have heard the rumors being whispered about you, have you not? They have only begun these last few days and–"

Scowling, Daniel shrugged as the music from the ball swirled around him.

"I do not care what society has to say about me. I am soon to leave London anyway, with no intention of returning unless it is for business."

Lord Milthorpe's eyebrows lifted.

"I have not enlightened you to my present state of mind, I know," Daniel continued, speaking quickly to get the explanation out as fast as he could, "but I have realized how much of a part the *ton* played in what happened with Lord

Newforth. Had he not been able to use society's inclination towards gossip and the like against Isabella, then she would not have been in such a difficulty." He put one hand on his friend's shoulder for a moment. "That is not to say that I am at all displeased with the betrothal, you understand. I see that Isabella has grown in her fondness for you and I shall always be very grateful indeed for what you did in stepping in and offering your hand. I am more than contented with the match, I assure you."

"I understand what you mean." Lord Milthorpe's frown grew heavier. "Though does this now mean that you intend to care nothing whatsoever for what the *ton* says of you? You must know that it will affect Isabella."

Daniel shook his head.

"Not in any severe way, I am sure. The *ton* is excited about her betrothal ball and, thereafter, there will be the wedding to plan. Once you are wed – which will not be more than a few months away – then I shall return to my estate and stay there. I have no desire to be a part of the *ton* any longer, given just how much darkness and shadow there is within it. I will pull myself from that as best I can and, once I am settled at my country estate, all shall be well. I will care nothing about whether or not society whispers about me. I shall spend my time in much more suitable endeavors and pursuits."

Lord Milthorpe ran one hand over his chin.

"And what of your own situation?"

"Situation?"

His friend nodded.

"You are unwed. You will require a match soon, will you not? You have the heir to produce." This was a thought that had not come to Daniel's mind at any point thus far and it gave him pause. "And this manner of yours, where it is noticeable to everyone that you have pulled away from the *ton* and are now appearing ill-tempered and disagreeable, does that not concern you also, as regards any future connection with a lady of society?"

"I... I had not thought of that."

"You have not danced a single dance this evening, nor at the last three balls we have attended," Lord Milthorpe continued, his words seeming to sink into Daniel's soul, weighing him down. "That has been noticed by society and, even though you say that you do not wish to be a part of the *ton* any longer – something that I can understand – that does mean that you might be making any future connections a little difficult."

Daniel chewed the edge of his lip, his brow furrowing.

"That is not something I have considered," he said, rubbing one hand over his face. "But I cannot say that I wish for a bride at any time soon. It could be that I retreat to my estate and, in some years, return to London to find a bride. I am sure that society will have no interest in me then."

Lord Milthorpe snorted and rolled his eyes.

"Do you really believe that the *ton* will have forgotten? It is a beast with a long memory, my friend. Whispers and rumors can continue for years! Do you not recall Lord and Lady Harrington? When he was to wed, the *ton* reminded us of just how much of a philanderer his late father was, whispering that *he* would, no doubt, take after him in the same way! It did not do his betrothed any good whatsoever, though they did still marry in the end."

Another reason that I dislike society, Daniel thought to himself, letting out a long breath.

"I cannot bring myself to be contented with all that society has to offer, not now that I have realized just how much difficulty it brings, how much darkness there is in the gossip and the whispers it so often clings to."

"Then what are you to do?"

"Oh, Lord Hastings! I am sure that you must have seen it, but we are all *eager* to know what it is that you think of it!"

A bright, much too loud voice forced Daniel's attention away from his present conversation and he turned his head, looking straight down into the eyes of Lady Hannah, a lady whom he had been acquainted with, some time ago. She was standing with two other young ladies, one of whom was giggling behind her fan and the other who did not seem to know where to look, given the way her gaze darted about.

He cleared his throat, a trifle irritated.

"I do not know what you mean."

"The London Chronicle!" Lady Hannah exclaimed, one hand reaching out to touch his arm lightly as her eyes twinkled. "Surely you must have seen it! I thought it a wonderful likeness."

"Especially since you have been rather... brooding of late," said the lady with the fan, her words a little muffled but reaching Daniel's ears, nonetheless. He scowled, turning his head sharply to look into Lord Milthorpe's face but his friend only shrugged, clearly as lost as Daniel was.

"I do not know of what you speak."

Lady Hannah giggled, the other two ladies joining her in their teasing laughter.

"Then might I suggest, Lord Hastings, that you find a copy of The London Chronicle and look for yourself?"

Daniel twisted on his heel without a word and strode to the ballroom door. He would, no doubt, be able to find The London Chronicle here in the house, though it would not be in the ballroom. He would be best to find the butler. His stomach twisted sharply as he thought about what might be contained within, beginning to worry that the drawing – for that was what it surely must be – had captured him in a less than kind manner. He did not know who the artist was but, he considered, it must be the same one, who had captured his sister and Lord Milthorpe in such a perfect likeness.

"You there." Seeing a footman, he held up one hand. "I require a copy of The London Chronicle. At once, if you please."

"Whatever are you doing?"

Daniel turned, just as the footman scurried off.

"I want to know what those ladies were speaking of."

Lord Milthorpe shrugged.

"It will just be a drawing of you, as there was of myself and your sister. Why does it matter what it is? You will see it soon enough - does it need to be this evening?"

A curl of worry rose in Daniel's stomach as he remembered the glitter that had been in Lady Hannah's eyes.

"There were remarks made," he muttered, beginning to pace up and down the hallway as Lord Milthorpe rolled his eyes. "One of them said I was brooding."

"But you have been," Lord Milthorpe pointed out, with a heavy sigh that told Daniel of his exasperation. "Besides which, I do not understand why you should care. Have you not only just finished informing me that you care nothing about society? That you want to step back from it?"

"I do not want to be mocked," Daniel answered, spinning on his heel and then looking Lord Milthorpe directly in the eye. "Do you not understand? This is precisely what I have been speaking of! Why am I the focus of this artist, whoever it is? There must be a purpose behind it. It cannot be merely that it has been done out of some vague artistic interest."

"My Lord."

The footman returned just as Daniel finished speaking and, after snatching the newspaper from the man's hand, Daniel made his way to a quieter part of the hallway, Lord Milthorpe hurrying after him. His heart was beginning to pound as he turned one page and then the next, only then to pause.

There.

The drawing was of him, just as he had suspected. He was standing with his back to the wall of a room, a heaviness in his frame and his head a little bowed, though his eyes were sharp, fixed on something ahead of him. Daniel blinked, trying to think of when he might have been seen in such a stance, only for his gaze to travel to the few short sentences below the drawing.

'There can be little doubt in the mind of the reader as to who this gentleman is! We have all noticed the darkness of his demeanor of late, the way he has shrunk back from all of us. What is all the more surprising is that this has come in the wake of his sister's joyous betrothal! Could it be jealousy that has driven the Viscount into the shadows? Or is there something else that troubles him?'

Daniel read the lines four times in a row before letting out a long, slow breath, fighting against the cresting anger that rose within him. This artist, whoever it was, had not only captured his visage, but also thought to write about his character! As a result, there would soon be whispers and rumors spreading around London about him, all the more! Closing his eyes, his jaw set tight, Daniel heard the newspaper crumple in his fist, his fury soon overwhelming him.

"Might I?"

Struggling to release the newspaper, Daniel finally opened his eyes, exhaled, and then offered it to Lord

Milthorpe. He watched as his friend read the lines and then frowned before, much to Daniel's irritation, he shrugged as though there was very little here to concern him.

"You have seen it now, yes?" Lord Milthorpe set The London Chronicle aside. "Might we now return to the ball? Your sister is with your mother at present, but I am very soon to dance with her, and I do not want to be tardy."

Throwing up his hands, Daniel glared at his friend.

"How can you say such a thing? How can you show so little concern?"

Lord Milthorpe's eyebrows lifted.

"I beg your pardon?"

"This artist, whoever it is, has chosen to write about me in a manner which is not only unfair but entirely improper."

Lord Milthorpe shrugged.

"It is only a few remarks and, quite frankly, none of them are untrue."

"But they ought not to be speaking about me for even a moment!" Daniel exclaimed, suddenly mortified. "I do not want the *ton* to say even a single thing about me!"

"I am afraid that you cannot control that, as well you know." Lord Milthorpe sniffed and then turned away. "Now, I am going to find Isabella. What is it that you wish to do, Hastings?"

Daniel glared down at the drawing as though, somehow, it was responsible for his present state of upset.

"I shall find the artist," he grated, his anger growing steadily. "And I shall demand to know what their intention was in not only drawing me but in writing such things about me." His expression still tight, he looked up again at Lord Milthorpe. "*That* is what I intend to do, Milthorpe. And I intend do to it now."

CHAPTER EIGHT

"I thank you, Lord Victorson." Patience smiled and then took back her dance card. "I look forward to stepping out with you."

The gentleman smiled, nodded, and then stepped away, leaving Patience to look after him, her lips lifting into a gentle smile. Lord Victorson was one of many gentlemen seeking to dance with her at this ball and Patience was rather pleased that she had done so well.

"And just how many dances do you have remaining?"

Patience chuckled as Christina took her dance card from her.

"I have only one dance remaining and it is the waltz."

"And no one has thought to take that from you as yet?" Christina's eyebrows lifted. "I would have thought, given the amount of interest in you at present, you might have had many gentlemen eager to take the waltz from you."

"Alas, they have not." Patience smiled as she took the dance card back from her sister. "But I do not know what it is that has made so many of them come to seek me out! It is most unusual, I confess."

"Do you not know?" Christina's eyebrows lifted. "It is the drawing you placed in The London Chronicle! I have heard many people speak of it this evening."

At this, Patience's eyebrows drew together.

"But I did ask them not to state that I was responsible for it," she said, a little confused. "How then…?" Her eyes closed as understanding came to her. "Ah. Eleanor." When she opened her eyes, Christina was looking away, a light pink on her cheeks. Patience's heart jumped in surprise. "And you also?"

"I could not help it!" her voice sounding a little like a whine, Christina spread out her hands and then let them fall to her sides. "I heard that Eleanor had been speaking of it and thus, I could not help myself! I wanted the *ton* to know that it was you, for there were so many compliments and the like that I could not help but speak!"

Patience closed her eyes again and let out a slow breath, trying to ignore the slight panic that made her whole being tremble just a little.

"I see." Looking around the ballroom, she felt herself shudder again. "Do you mean to say that most of the *ton* here this evening know that I am the one who has drawn the figure of Lord Hastings and, before that, Lord Milthorpe and Miss Spearton?"

"Yes!" Christina clapped her hands lightly, then beamed at Patience as though this was something truly wonderful. "There have been so many remarks made, and great delight in all that you have drawn, I can assure you! That is why, I hope, that these gentlemen have come to seek you out. It is because they are impressed with your talents, with your skill! I think that you should be heartened by this, my dear sister."

Patience swallowed hard, trying not to give in to the

panic that clutched at her. She looked around at the *ton* again, seeing them now with different eyes. The glances given to her were knowing looks, clearly stating that they knew that *she* was the one who had drawn these things, that *she* was the one who was now becoming known for her work in The London Chronicle.

"You should not look so afraid!" Christina exclaimed, putting one hand on Patience's arm. "This is wonderful, is it not? You have gentlemen seeking you out now, ready to pursue you, to take you into their company *because* of the talent they have seen in you. Why, then, do you still look so troubled? There can be nothing of concern here, truly."

"I wish I felt the same confidence as you," Patience answered, her chest a little tight still. "I am worried that there will be those who are displeased with what I have done, who will make their feelings well known to society."

Christina shrugged.

"I think that these people are very few, Patience. Come now, you have only one dance left, and it is the waltz, is it not? I am sure that you will be able to have it taken by another *marvelous* gentleman by the time it comes to it. Put the news that I have told you out of your mind and do not concern yourself with it any longer." Linking arms with her, Christina half pulled Patience away from where she stood, forcing her to walk with her. "This is an excellent thing," she said again, as Patience took in slow and steadying breaths. "All will be well. This evening will be the best ball that you have enjoyed thus far, I am quite sure of it."

If only I could be so, Patience thought to herself, biting the edge of her lip. *But I cannot be sure that everyone will think well of it... and I wonder what Lord Hastings himself thinks of what I have done.*

"Lady Patience?"

Having had no success in filling her waltz, Patience turned with an expectant smile on her face, hoping that whichever gentleman this was might have come to her in the hope of stepping out for the waltz, given that it was just about to be announced. Instead, she saw the angry expression of Lord Hastings, his eyes almost shooting fire, his jaw tight, and his eyebrows low and heavy, sending shadows across his expression.

Her stomach lurched.

"It was *you*!" One finger pointed towards her, his hand reaching out as Patience took a step back, her eyes widening. "*You* did this."

Patience opened her mouth, struggling to form her words.

"I – I do not–"

"Ah, good evening, Lord Hastings. You may not recall, but we were introduced some days ago, though you are already acquainted with my daughter, I understand."

Instantly, Lord Hastings' hand fell back to his side, and he began to splutter as Patience's mother came to stand beside her, sending a curious look towards Patience before returning her attention to the Viscount.

"Yes, yes, of course. Good evening," Lord Hastings managed to say, though his words were quick and forced, and he was struggling to speak with any sort of calmness. "Lady Osterley, I was just–"

"How wonderful that you have come to ask my daughter for the waltz!"

Patience's stomach twisted and she snatched in a

breath, her eyes flaring as she turned to her mother, though Lady Osterley ignored her entirely, keeping her attention fixed on Lord Hastings.

"I – I was not..."

"It is the only dance that has not yet been taken, for I fear that many gentlemen have believed that I have not yet given Patience permission to dance the waltz, but she has every permission she might wish for!"

Lady Osterley laughed brightly, but Patience only shook her head, not wanting her mother to force either herself or Lord Hastings into a dance that neither of them wanted.

"Mama, I am sure that–"

"What is it, Patience?" Lady Osterley finally turned her head and looked into Patience's eyes, a slight lift to one of her eyebrows. "Is there something wrong? Surely Lord Hastings cannot have come to you in such a forward manner for *any* other reason than to seek out your waltz?"

Patience did not know what to say in response to this. Her mother had seen the forceful manner in which Lord Hastings had approached her, and the last thing she wished to do was to state that she believed Lord Hastings was coming to berate her in some severe fashion. That would only cause a good deal of difficulty and embarrassment for both herself, *and* for Lord Hastings, when things were already difficult enough.

"I..." Lord Hastings had suddenly gone very pale, the upset that had ballooned in him instantly deflating, making him appear a little smaller than he had initially seemed to Patience. "Yes, of course. The waltz." He cleared his throat, looking about. "It is to be announced, yes?"

"It has only just *been* announced!" Lady Osterley

beamed at him, though Patience felt herself sinking inside. "Thank you, Lord Hastings. This has made Patience's ball a truly excellent one, for she will have danced every dance this evening now!"

Lord Hastings forced a smile, though Patience could still see the shadows in his eyes. Inclining his head, he offered her his arm.

"Lady Patience, shall we?"

She took a breath but, aware that she had no choice but to accept, placed her hand on his arm and, thereafter, fell into step with him. She could practically feel the tension radiating from him, the strength of his frame overwhelming her. Soon, she was to be held in his arms, and what would that feel like? Would his anger burn through her then also?

"I know that you do not wish to dance the waltz," she whispered, a little hoarsely. "You must forgive my mother. She was a little forward, I know, but–"

"Shall we dance, Lady Patience?" Lord Hastings interrupted, his jaw jutting forward as he looked directly into her eyes. "Mayhap what it is that I have to say can be spoken during our dance."

Without warning, Patience was swept into his arms, having not realized that the music had begun. She gasped, struggling to find her composure as Lord Hastings began to lead her around the floor, his arm firm at her waist, the other hand grasping hers with a strength that she had not expected. It felt like an age as they danced together, without a word, and Patience fought for every breath, trying to find a sense of balance within herself but struggling all the same.

"The drawing." Finally, Lord Hastings spoke, his voice low and grating. "That was your work."

Patience tried to look into his face but found the dark

intensity of his gaze to be a little overwhelming. Instead of answering him, she chose to remain silent, feeling it a little foolish to answer a question that he already knew the answer to.

"What made you think that to do such a thing was wise?" he asked, pulling her a little closer as her breath tumbled out of her chest in a rushed, hurried fashion. "Did you seek to make me a laughingstock?"

Patience's eyes flared.

"Of course not."

"Then why would you do such a thing?"

Confusion raged within her as Patience looked back at him, finding it easier now to hold his gaze, her steps managing to be in time with his without any real difficulty, which surprised her.

"I only drew you, Lord Hastings. I did not think that you would be in the least bit upset by it."

His hand tightened on her for only a moment, a flush of color in his cheeks as he turned his head away sharply, seeming to not know what to say in response to what she had said. Patience's heart quickened, and she was utterly confused about why he appeared to be so deeply upset with her artwork. Yes, she had been concerned that not everyone would appreciate her artwork and yes, she had been a little worried over what the *ton* would think of her drawing being published in The London Chronicle, but Lord Hastings was speaking as though she had personally insulted him in some way by doing so.

"It was only a drawing, Lord Hastings," she said, managing to lift her chin just a little. "It was not my idea to have my work printed in The London Chronicle, it was the thought of another, though, if my drawing of you has been truly upsetting, then I shall mayhap think carefully about offering up another for printing."

Lord Hastings said nothing. Instead, he continued to dance, but in complete silence, looking down at her and holding her gaze with a steadiness that confused Patience a great deal. Why was it that he appeared so very upset? What was it about the drawing that had caused him to think of it as an insult? It was not as though she had drawn him in her usual style, exaggerating any of his features. Instead, it had simply been as she had remembered him.

What could be so insulting about that?

"I am truly sorry." As the music came to a close, Patience stepped back from Lord Hastings, relieved to be free from him. "I had no intention of upsetting you. My only hope was that the *ton* – and you– might appreciate what I had done. That is all."

Lord Hastings snorted and shook his head, making Patience flush with embarrassment, looking away as she bobbed a quick curtsey. Evidently, he did not believe her, though she could not understand why that might be. What was it that she had done which caused him such disbelief?

"Thank you for dancing with me and for tolerating my mother's determination," she murmured, making to step back. "I think that–"

"You must know that I cannot believe you."

Patience turned back to face Lord Hastings, who ambled towards her with his hands behind his back, forcing her to fall into step with him rather than make her way away from him.

"You could never have had such a thing printed without intention," he said, his eyes narrowing just a little. "As I have said, Lady Patience, I cannot believe that there was no ill intent." His shoulders lifted and then fell. "I do hope that you will find a way to be truthful with me as to your motivations, Lady Patience, for I simply cannot understand it. We are barely acquainted, we have shared only one or two conversations and yes, I will admit to being a little brusque, but you cannot use that as a reason for such dark words."

"Words?" Nonplussed, Patience stopped and turned to look at him, but Lord Hastings only snorted and then stepped away from her, leaving Patience to stare after him. It took her a few moments but, eventually, she made her way back to the other guests, hurrying to find her mother, sister, or cousin in the hope that she might stand with one of them.

Words? Patience bit her lip, her thoughts going round and round in her mind with a frantic haste which made her stomach twist sharply. *What words does he speak of? I have said nothing of him.*

"Patience? Are you quite all right? I saw you dancing with Lord Hastings and–"

"Have you seen The London Chronicle since it was printed?" Grasping Eleanor's hand, Patience threw up her other hand. "You *must* have seen it. What else was there?"

Confusion grew in her cousin's eyes.

"What else?"

"Lord Hastings danced with me, yes, but not for the reasons you might think." Closing her eyes, Patience took a steadying breath and then tried to speak calmly, without permitting the worry which ran through her veins to capture her. "He was deeply upset. He asked me about my reasons for doing such a thing, stating that I must have had some dark intentions and, thereafter, said something about the words there? I do not know what he meant."

Eleanor nodded, no concern in her eyes.

"Yes, there were a few short sentences written in the paper, just after your drawing," she said, making Patience's eyebrows lift. "But that was not written by you, of course."

"No, it was not." The worry in Patience's thoughts now began to grow. "What did it say, Eleanor? Was it anything terrible?"

Her cousin's face screwed up for a moment as she tried to remember.

"I – I do not recall exactly, but it was something about his demeanor and stance, just as you had drawn it. He certainly *has* changed somewhat these last few weeks, and that was noted by whoever wrote the sentences underneath your drawing."

Patience let out a slow breath and then shook her head, a lump growing in her throat.

"And he thinks that *I* was the one responsible, not only for the drawing but for the words written about him. That is why he was so upset."

"Yes, I presume that might be why," Eleanor replied, speaking slowly as though she was a little confused, "but that is to be expected. It is not as though anything that was said there was untrue."

"I must see the paper." Patience rubbed one hand over her eyes. "We must find a copy so that I can read it."

A hand touched her arm lightly.

"Patience? It is time for us to take our leave. Your sister is fatigued and now that the waltz is completed, I think it would be wise to make our way home."

Patience shook her head.

"Mama, I must speak with Lord Hastings. It is important."

Lady Osterley's eyebrows lifted.

"Lord Hastings?"

"Not for any significant reason," Patience clarified quickly, not wishing her mother to think that there was anything untoward – or exciting – about Patience's desire to speak with the gentleman. "There has been a misunderstanding, I think, and I must seek to clarify it."

"That cannot be done tonight."

Patience swallowed tightly.

"Mama, please. It is important."

Lady Osterley searched Patience's expression but then shook her head no.

"It has been a long evening, and everyone is fatigued, Patience. Whatever it is that is concerning you, I am sure that it can be dealt with at another time. If you wish, I can go with you to call on him tomorrow."

Frustration and upset sent tears into Patience's eyes, but she blinked them away, refusing to let her mother see them. She wanted to argue, wanted to demand that her mother permit her to do as she wished, but instead, Patience kept her mouth closed and chose to remain entirely silent. She could not be selfish at this moment, could not only think of herself, though her worry grew with every passing moment. She wanted to turn and run through the ballroom, find Lord Hastings, and cling to his arm as she told him the truth, that she had not been the one to write any of those words beneath the drawing... but she could not.

At the very least, I can write to The London Chronicle and beg them to make it clear that I have not written what goes beneath each drawing. She closed her eyes, her chest tight. *Though if only I could speak with Lord Hastings this evening! I would make everything quite plain and all would be well.*

It would have to wait for another time, though whether

or not Lord Hastings would even speak with her, Patience could not tell. Mayhap he would reject every offer of her company, and would think ill of her for the rest of the Season, and though she could not understand why, it felt as though that might be the very worst thing that could happen.

CHAPTER NINE

Muttering to himself, Daniel made his way into White's and, snapping his fingers at one of the footmen, sat down heavily in a chair near a fireplace which, much to his relief, had glowing embers within it. He had not attended any occasion this evening, having chosen to step away from society entirely. Last evening's ball had been the most dreadful of the Season, for he had learned that he had not only his likeness published in The London Chronicle, but also a statement about his character which, he now knew, everyone in the *ton* had read. Quite what had possessed Lady Patience to write such things about him, he did not know, but he felt more than a little foolish because of it.

The truth was, he had thought well of the lady. He had considered her a fine young woman who had interrupted his conversation with Lord Newforth to save embarrassment to both himself and, thereafter, to Isabella. There had been a spark of interest within him also, appreciating her warm smile and the way that the candlelight had danced across her golden curls. Yes, even when they had been forced into dancing the waltz together, he had taken note of her beauty, even though he had been coldly furious about all that she had done.

Foolish.

Accepting the glass of brandy from the footman with a nod, Daniel did not lift it to his lips right away, but watched it swirl around the glass. The more he learned about society, the less he valued it. It was an enemy, something to be careful of, to guard against. It was a lesson learned much too late, he considered, though now, of course, he was faced with a dilemma.

How am I to find a bride if I reject society, as I had intended?

Rubbing one hand down his face, Daniel let out a sigh, and then finally took a sip of his brandy. Lord Milthorpe's questions had been a trifle irritating, but he had made Daniel consider some things in a way that he had not before. Yes, there *was* a responsibility for him to find a bride and continue the family line, and yes, he might be unable to do that if he pushed himself away from society with the determination that he had intended.

"But what am I to do?"

Muttering to himself again, Daniel closed his eyes and rested his head back against the chair. How could he find a bride while, at the same time, making sure that he did not involve himself in society as he wanted?

"You have decided not to join society this evening, I see."

Daniel's eyes flew open, his whole body tensing as he turned his head, only to see Lord Newforth grinning darkly down at him. His jaw set and he turned his head away, choosing not to answer. As far as he was concerned, Lord Newforth was not a gentleman he had any interest in speaking with, and he wanted to make that very clear indeed.

"You are not going to ignore me, are you?" Lord Newforth chuckled, but the sound did not bring any lightness to Daniel's spirit. "I thought that we might speak together, Lord Hastings."

"I have nothing that I wish to say to you." Daniel kept his head turned, his gaze steady and fixed. "Good evening, Lord Newforth."

The gentleman only laughed again, and Daniel gritted his teeth, refusing to permit himself to say anything more to him. Lord Newforth seemed quite determined to be in Daniel's company, though Daniel was quite certain that this would not be for any good reason.

"You know that I have every intention of bringing down dark consequences upon your head for what you did in keeping your sister from me." Lord Newforth set one hand on Daniel's shoulder and squeezed, hard. "Are you afraid, Lord Hastings? Are you always watching for me, wondering what it is that I will do?" He lifted his hand from Daniel's shoulder and then came around to face him. "Is *that* why you have pulled away from all of society?"

Daniel snorted.

"My actions have nothing whatsoever to do with you, Lord Newforth."

"Are you sure?"

The melodious, mocking manner in which Lord Newforth spoke made Daniel's anger flare all the hotter and he turned his head away, his free hand curled tightly into a fist though, again, he chose to remain silent. It was better for him to say nothing, to let Lord Newforth say whatever it was that he wished, before going on his way - for to react in fury and upset would only give Lord Newforth what he so clearly desired.

"You must be aware that I have every intention of injuring you as much as I possibly can." Lord Newforth tipped his head. "You *are* afraid, are you not?" He laughed and Daniel closed his eyes for a moment in an attempt to hold himself back from saying the furious, dark things he wished to spit back at Lord Newforth. "I am glad of it, Lord Hastings, for there is much that I can, and will, do to you. I may not have been able to take Isabella as my bride, as I wished, but there are other means by which I can injure you, and improve my own standing at the very same time." With a chuckle, he tilted his head. "In fact, I have already begun."

"What do you mean by that?" Unable to hold back the question from his lips, Daniel slammed the brandy glass down on the table next to him and threw himself to his feet. "If you are intending to threaten me, then I can assure you that *nothing* you say will make any difference whatsoever. I have already pulled my sister away from you and her happiness is all that matters to me."

"Ah, but what of your own happiness?" Lord Newforth answered, a sly smile still curving his lips. "And what if *her* happiness can be tainted in some way? Yes, she might well be betrothed, and I presume the marriage will go ahead as it ought, but that does not mean that all will be well. There is still a great deal that can go wrong. A great deal that can injure both you and your sister, Lord Hastings. And if I were you, then I should be a good deal more careful about every step you take."

Daniel wanted to reach out and grasp Lord Newforth's

collar, to shake him, hard, until his teeth rattled and all of his secrets came pouring out. His determination to stay back and remain silent was beginning to fail, and he let out a low growl and then took a step forward – but Lord Newforth only laughed and spun on his heel before striding away from him. Seething inwardly, Daniel watched the man with narrowed eyes, wondering what it was that Lord Newforth had been threatening and, at the same time, fearing for both himself and Isabella. What was it that Newforth intended to do? Surely it would not be to break apart the betrothal in some dreadful way? Panic gripped him hard for a moment and, sitting down, he picked up his brandy glass and drained it in one swallow.

He cannot break their betrothal, he told himself, shutting his eyes as he took in slow breaths to counter his racing heart. *And both Lord Milthorpe and I are watching Isabella carefully. She is quite safe.*

His eyes opened.

So then it is I who must be wary. Who must be ready for whatever he intends.

Swallowing, Daniel shook his head and then snapped his fingers at another footman. Lord Newforth was quite clear in his intentions, which was extraordinary in itself! To have a fellow state, quite plainly, that his only thought was to injure him was extraordinary though, also, in its own way, a little frightening. With a knot in his throat, he ordered another brandy before sinking back down into his chair, his eyes on the glowing embers in the fire as a good many heavy thoughts pulled at his mind.

∽

Daniel scowled and quickly turned his gaze away from the group of young ladies who had been drawing near. Having spent the previous evening at White's and then the rest of the night tossing and turning in his bed, Daniel had woken with a fresh determination. He was *not* about to let Lord Newforth frighten him, nor deter him from doing whatever he wished. No, he would not hide himself away in his townhouse for fear of what Lord Newforth would do, and nor would he say anything to Isabella. Daniel was now determined to believe that all that Lord Newforth had said was nothing but lies, said to upset Daniel and fill his mind with concern – but he was *not* going to let the man succeed.

Thus, he had stepped out and had chosen to wander through the streets of London, thinking mayhap to choose a new book from the bookshop or perhaps stop at Gunter's for an ice. Yes, Lord Newforth might be present and yes, he might very well see him, but if he did, then what of it? It would only prove to Lord Newforth that what he had tried to do had, yet again, failed utterly. Now, however, it was not Lord Newforth's face that concerned Daniel. Instead, it was that of Lady Patience, the young lady who had not only drawn him in such a recognizable fashion, but had also chosen to write about him and state, to all who read the paper, just what she thought of his character. If he was not mistaken, she was amongst that group of young ladies who were approaching. The urge to turn away directly so that she would neither see him nor wish to speak with him was severe and, after a moment or two, Daniel gave into it. One swift movement later, and he was in a small establishment which, to his eyes, appeared to sell nothing but buttons and ribbons.

He groaned inwardly, though he kept his head high all

the same. He had chosen poorly when it came to where he was to hide himself, for this shop held nothing for him.

"Good afternoon, my Lord." The shopkeeper came towards him, a slightly older lady with a warm smile. "Might I be of any assistance? Are you purchasing something for perhaps your mother, sister, or wife?"

Daniel blinked quickly, then cast a glance over his shoulder. Much to his frustration, the group of young ladies had come to a stop directly outside the shop which meant he could not hurry back outside. Clearing his throat, he put his hands behind his back and attempted a smile. "My sister is recently betrothed."

The shopkeeper's eyes flared, her smile wide.

"How wonderful! Might I enquire as to her name?"

"Miss Spearton." Daniel frowned as the lady's smile slipped. "I have recently sent out invitations to her betrothal ball, and I thought I ought to purchase her a little gift for it."

"I see." The shopkeeper gestured to all of the various items within her shop. "If you wish to peruse all that I have here, Lord Hastings, then I would be glad to assist you, should you have any questions."

Daniel blinked quickly, recognizing that the shopkeeper had spoken his name without him once introducing himself. A slow flush crept into his face as he realized that she must have read The London Chronicle, and recognized him from that. With a sharp nod, he turned away at once, only for the bell to ring as the door behind him opened.

"Good afternoon, my lady." The shopkeeper's welcoming words were spoken to the new customer. "Is there anything you might wish to look for today? I would be glad to help you."

"I thank you."

Daniel heard nothing more that was said, cringing

inwardly as he recognized the voice. It was none other than the very lady he had sought to escape – and now would have to face.

Lady Patience had, seemingly inadvertently, followed him into the shop, and now he would have to speak with her, whether he wished it or not.

CHAPTER TEN

*P*atience smiled at the shopkeeper, thinking her very amiable indeed.

"I thank you. I think that I shall look at the ribbons, as I should very much like a new one for an upcoming ball."

"But of course. I am more than able to help you, should you require it."

With a nod of thanks, Patience made her way across the shop to where the ribbons were all laid out, only to spy another person standing within that area. It was, to her surprise, a gentleman - and this immediately made her a little ill at ease. It would not be right to be in this space without any chaperone, though her mother was immediately outside, standing in conversation with Lady Pearson and Eleanor. She went to pull her gaze away, only for the gentleman to look a little to the right – and Patience's breath hitched. Before she could even think about what to do, she found her legs carrying her towards him, her relief palpable.

"Lord Hastings, thank goodness I have been able to find you!"

The gentleman did not look in the least bit pleased to

see her, however. He turned, his lip curling a little as he looked into her eyes.

"Lady Patience, I do not think that we have anything more to say to each other. Good afternoon."

"No, no, please!" Without meaning to, Patience reached out and managed to catch his hand with hers. Knowing that it was more than a little inappropriate to do so, she held onto it regardless, her breathing growing quick and fast as he looked into her face in evident surprise at her actions. She did not dare let him go for fear that he would stride away from her, and her opportunity to explain herself leave with him. "I must speak with you. Please, I beg of you to listen for only a moment."

Lord Hastings went suddenly very still, her fingers pressing his as her heart pounded in her chest. He swallowed hard, his throat bobbing as he gazed into her eyes, seeming to soften directly in front of her.

"I suppose I am able to trust that you, at the very least, have nothing to do with Lord Newforth."

Confused, Patience blinked but said nothing, not understanding in the least what he meant. A few more moments of silence came, only for Lord Hastings to shrug.

"Very well, Lady Patience. What is it that you have to say?"

Relief made her suddenly a little weak.

"I thank you," she breathed, still holding his hand. "Lord Hastings, you cannot know just how much I regret sending in the drawing to The London Chronicle. Had I known that someone else would have added to my drawing by writing those few lines, then I would never have consented for my work to be printed!" Lord Hastings's lips flattened, nothing else in his expression changing. Patience could not tell whether or not he believed her, nor even whether or not he understood a single thing she was saying. "I did not want to put my work into The London Chronicle at first, I assure you," she continued, coming a little closer to him. "It was suggested to me by another, and the first one I offered was of your sister and Lord Milthorpe."

"That had nothing written beneath it," Lord Hastings interrupted, as Patience nodded quickly. "Why did you choose not to write anything there?"

A frustrated breath rushed out of her.

"As I have said, I did not write anything, Lord Hastings. If you wish, you can write to The London Chronicle and ask who it was that wrote those sentences about you! I promise you, with every truth of my heart, that I did not write a single word. I would not do such a thing, for I can see that those words have caused you pain and upset, and I have no cause to want those things to injure you." A slight catch came into her voice, such was her determination to speak the truth and have him believe her. "I can understand that you have no other reason to believe me, aside from my telling you this, but my desperation to inform you of it must mean something, I assure you."

Blinking quickly, and a little embarrassed that her eyes were now growing damp, Patience could do nothing but gaze into his eyes and silently pray that what she had said would have an effect. Lord Hastings stood stock still, his dark green eyes flickering with questions, perhaps questions that he was asking, and Patience held her breath, waiting for him to finally respond.

Eventually – and much to her surprise – he put his other hand on top of their joined ones and let out a long, steady breath before dropping his head. Then, with another breath, he lifted his gaze and set his shoulders straight before, finally, his lips curved just a little.

"I believe you, Lady Patience."

"You do?" Patience, her relief overwhelming, took another step forward before stepping back again, mortified at the thought that had thrown itself at her – which was to fling her arms around his neck and hug him tightly. "I cannot tell you how much I am grateful for your trust in me, Lord Hastings."

"I believe you because of your fervor, Lady Patience."

Lord Hastings squeezed her hand and Patience, a flush on her face, smiled and then, after a moment, pulled her hand away. She had not really thought about what she was doing in holding Lord Hastings' hand, and certainly had not intended to hold it for so long! In her fervor, as Lord Hastings had called it, she had not even noticed it. Now, she could only pray that he did not think her improper!

"I am sorry that I rushed towards you in such a way," she said, only for Lord Hastings to chuckle.

"Given the way I rushed towards you at the ball, Lady Patience, you have no reason to apologize. I am the one who ought to apologize to you, which I shall do at this very moment." Putting one hand to his heart, he bowed towards her. "Forgive me for how I demanded to speak with you at the ball, Lady Patience. I was upset and, truth be told, quite angry at what had been said." He winced, looking away. "Not because there was no truth in it, as Lord Milthorpe has reminded me, but because I have found myself a little... less than pleased with society of late. I felt as though this was yet another way for them to whisper about me, reminding me of all that I have come to dislike about the *ton*. Though I am glad to hear that you had nothing to do with it, Lady Patience." He smiled, a brightness coming into his eyes which Patience had never seen before, making her heart jump in her chest. "Your work is quite remarkable. I know that my sister *and* Lord Milthorpe were both quite taken with your drawing of them. You captured something there that has given them a lot of hope."

Patience did not understand why hope was something that was needed in the seemingly happy betrothal between Lord Milthorpe and Miss Spearton but, all the same, she smiled at Lord Hastings, glad to hear the kindness in his voice.

"Thank you for your trust in me, Lord Hastings. It means a good deal to me to have you believe what I have said. You cannot know of the strain that bore down upon me when I realized what you thought! It is not at all as you believed, and I am greatly relieved to know that you can see that now."

"I can." With a smile, Lord Hastings gestured to the door. "Are you here with your mother and sister?"

"And Eleanor, my cousin," Patience answered, her heart beginning to slow from what had been a very frantic rhythm indeed. "And you? Are you here with your sister?"

He shook his head.

"No, I came alone."

"Ah." Her smile grew as she realized his reason for stepping into such an establishment. "Then you must be seeking out a gift for her."

Lord Hastings laughed softly, confusing Patience for a moment, only for him to nod. "Yes, yes, that is my *only* reason for being in such a place as this. For my mother too, mayhap, for the betrothal ball is soon to be upon us and I now think it would be very fitting for them to both receive a gift from me."

"I am sure that they would very much appreciate any sort of kindness from you in that regard, yes."

With a small tilt of his head, Lord Hastings seemed to

consider for a moment before, with a slight lift of his shoulders – as though he had not been certain about something – he smiled.

"Might you be willing to advise me, Lady Patience? I confess to knowing very little about such things as this."

With a grand sweep of his hand across the shop, he looked back at her, a hopeful glint in his eye.

"But of course!" Delighted to have been asked and seeing it as his way of assuring her that he took every word that she had said as truth, Patience turned to look at the many ribbons, buttons, lace, and more within the shop. "I would be more than delighted to help you. I am sure that we will be able to find something quite lovely that both your mother and your sister will adore."

CHAPTER ELEVEN

"Good evening."

Daniel inclined his head as Lord Gilmerton and his wife took their leave of him, relieved that the conversation had gone well. He had been bold and had chosen to step out into society again, despite Lord Newforth's warnings. After his conversation the previous day with Lady Patience, and his understanding that she had *not* written those words about him as he had thought, Daniel had been emboldened. Yes, he was still going to be careful and cautious and yes, he certainly was not about to fully step back into society, for his feelings on that remained the same, but neither was he about to hide himself away. It was not for his own sake that he did that, however, but solely for Isabella's who, at this very moment, was standing beside him, seemingly delighted with every moment of this ball.

"Your own betrothal ball is in a fortnight," Daniel murmured to her, her hand on his arm as they made their way around the ballroom, solely so that Isabella might nod and smile at others, though Daniel's expression remained somewhat fixed and a little clouded. "I do hope that it will go well for you, Isabella. You deserve to have nothing but honor and happiness."

"I am sure that it shall." Isabella smiled up at him, her eyes bright as the candlelight flickered across the copper in her hair. "Mama is pleased with the match, society is pleased with the match and, if I am to be entirely truthful, brother, I should say that I too am truly delighted with Lord Milthorpe."

Daniel stopped walking at once, pausing as he turned his head to look fully into his sister's eyes.

"I beg your pardon?" he said, speaking quietly, but with great deliberation as a hint of color came into his sister's face. "Are you trying to tell me that you are happy that you are betrothed to Lord Milthorpe? That the match is, to your mind, an excellent one?"

"It is better than Lord Newforth, certainly!" Isabella laughed, though the color in her face heightened all the more. After a short pause, she let out a soft sigh and then lifted her shoulders lightly. "If I am to be entirely truthful, then I should tell you that my heart has found itself quite contented with Milthorpe. He has long been a friend of mine, as he has been to you also, but there is something in our connection now which makes my interest and, indeed, my affection for him, grow steadily. You may think me a little foolish, for you have never thought or considered love or affection and things like that, but it has been vastly important to me."

Daniel put his hand over hers as it sat on his arm.

"You quite mistake me, my dear sister. It is not that I think any less of you or that I think you in the least bit foolish. Indeed, it is quite the opposite!"

"Oh?"

He smiled, his heart warming.

"I am glad, Isabella. Overjoyed, I think, to hear that you have found a happiness with Lord Milthorpe that you had always hoped for. I will be entirely honest and state that I am a little surprised, and that I did not expect such a thing, but all the same, I am very happy indeed to hear of it."

Isabella smiled brighter than he had seen her do in some time, her cheeks flushed, but stars seeming to fill her eyes.

"He is a wonderful man, Hastings. I did not ever think that there would be such a connection between us, but he has proven himself to me, from the very moment that he stepped in to stop Lord Newforth's dark intentions."

"He certainly has."

"Who has? And what has he done?"

Daniel chuckled as the very person they had been speaking about came to join them.

"You must have known that we were speaking of you, my friend, though what we said was all quite wonderful, I assure you."

"I am glad to hear it." Lord Milthorpe smiled into Isabella's eyes and Daniel's heart lifted at the joy which spread across Isabella's face. He went to step away, intending to leave Lord Milthorpe to spend some time with Isabella, only for his friend to look back at him. "Did you see The London Chronicle this morning?"

A slight frown touched Daniel's face.

"No, I did not."

"There is another drawing in it, and a few sentences written thereafter, though it has been made quite plain now that the writer and the artist are two different people - I do hope that brings you peace of mind."

Daniel winced.

"If the truth is to be told, I may have already learned

that fact from one Lady Patience, who came to beg of me to believe her. And the reason she did such a thing was because I went to her and practically demanded that she give me her reasons for writing those sentences about me." He shook his head as Isabella's eyes sharpened, clearly displeased with what he had done. "It appears that she was just as surprised as I to see those words written there."

"I do hope that you apologized." Isabella put both hands on her hips. "Goodness, I can already imagine the way in which you said those words to her!"

Looking away, Daniel cleared his throat, aware that he deserved Isabella's upset.

"I did. Of course I did."

Letting his mind go back to that moment when he had spoken to Lady Patience in the shop, he *also* remembered how she had caught his hand in hers. It had been unexpected, but at the same time, Daniel had found it somewhat... delightful. There had been something about her nearness, the hope shining in her eyes, and the warmth of her hand held fast in his that had made his heart suddenly yearn to be closer to her, though he had tried to untangle such desires quickly, confused by them. The desire to apologize had, of course, been legitimate, and he had felt deep shame over what he had done, and how he had acted, though Lady Patience had not held anything against him. Instead, she had been gracious and kind, helping him with his gifts for Isabella and his mother. The edge of his lip curled slightly as he thought of how her blonde curls had bounced gently as she had shown him one thing and the next, how her eyes had glowed with a sense of clear delight over a pair of new gloves, though Daniel had not truly understood her fascination. It had been on a whim that he had asked her for her help, and it had been a wise decision to do so. The time he had spent in her company – though it had not been overly long – had been delightful, and had brought him out of the darkness which he had held fast to for some time.

"Hastings?"

With a slight jerk, Daniel's eyes flared as he saw his sister and Lord Milthorpe exchange a look.

"Yes?"

"You were quite lost in thought." Isabella's eyebrows lifted lightly. "Was there something specific that was occupying your thoughts?"

Daniel shook his head no, having no desire to disclose that he had been thinking solely of Lady Patience.

"Then shall we–"

"*There* he is."

A loud voice made Daniel spin around, astonished that someone should think to behave in such an ill manner, only for something hard to thump into his chest, pushing him back. He stumbled, caught by his sister and Lord Milthorpe as he fought to gain an understanding of what was happening.

"You owe me a great deal of money." A gentleman that Daniel did not recognize, a tall, broad-shouldered, and angry fellow, pointed one thick finger in Daniel's direction. "Did you think you could run from my establishment and do nothing about paying the debts you owe?"

"Establishment?" Daniel frowned, irritated not only by the gentleman's physical actions but by the words coming out of his mouth – words that could be heard by a good many others. "I do not know what it is that you are speaking of."

"You know very well what I speak!" Daniel took a closer look at the fellow, sensing a slight loss of refinement in the gentleman's manner. Who was he? And what establishment was he speaking of? "You were there yesterday afternoon!" the gentleman bellowed, making a few heads turn. "You enjoyed your time with my ladies, drank a good deal, and then left the place before paying me a single penny!"

Heat poured into Daniel's face as all of those who had been listening suddenly began to whisper to one another, as others too then came a little closer to Daniel and the gentleman, clearly eager to hear what it was that was being said.

"Yesterday?" Daniel drew himself up, determined now to defend himself. "You are quite mistaken, sir. I have not been in your establishment and, indeed, do not even know what it is that you speak of!"

The gentleman let out a roar of evident rage, his eyes narrowing into sharp slits.

"How dare you give such a pretense, Lord Hastings? You know my establishment very well! If I have to, I can get one of the ladies there to confirm that you were present with us yesterday afternoon, but that you had to depart in the evening to attend some soiree or ball or some such thing."

Certain now that all of those who listened were sure that this fellow was speaking of a house of ill repute, Daniel swallowed hard.

"You are mistaken, sir." His chin lifted, his hands balling tight. "It was not I who was present there. I have never frequented such a place and never shall."

"Then where were you, Lord Hastings?"

The voice of Lord Newforth sent a prickling heat cascading down Daniel's back as he sent a hard, angry look in the gentleman's direction, aware that *he* was the reason that this fellow had chosen to come and bellow such dreadful things. Lord Newforth had arranged it all, determined now that he would do whatever he could to shame Daniel in front of all of society.

Except Daniel was not about to permit him to do so.

"I was walking through London," he said, firmly. "I frequented a shop and thereafter, returned home. I did attend a card party last evening, however, and was seen there by a good many people."

"But that is not what is being asked." Lord Newforth tilted his head just a little. "It is not the evening that is being spoken of for, as you say, you were seen at this card party. It is the afternoon and all you can offer us is that you were in *one* single shop, and nothing more?"

Daniel's jaw tightened as he glared at Lord Newforth. Evidently, the gentleman had done a great deal of careful consideration and study, seeing where Daniel had been in the evening and recognizing that to declare him at some dark establishment at that time would do no good. Thus, he had settled on the afternoon.

"I think that you will find that I was seen by a good few members of the *ton* yesterday afternoon, Lord Newforth," he said, as calmly but as decisively as he could, turning his head to look into the other gentleman's face. "I am afraid that I do not even know your name, sir, but I can assure you that you are mistaken."

"I cannot be mistaken!" The large, angry fellow took a step closer to Daniel, his eyes narrowing. "I know your face, I know the name you gave me and–"

"Someone might very well have been using my name for their own purposes," Daniel interrupted quickly, catching the scowl that ran into Lord Newforth's expression at this statement. Perhaps this was precisely what had been done, Daniel considered, and Lord Newforth was now quite frustrated that his actions had been understood so easily. "You are mistaken, good sir. I was not at your establishment, and I do not owe you any money."

Lord Newforth sniffed, spreading out his hands.

"We can all understand why you might wish to defend yourself, Lord Hastings, for there are so many of us here – and so many listening – but that is only *your* word. If you were out in London yesterday afternoon, then you must have been in company with someone? There must have been many who saw you, yes?"

Daniel opened his mouth to speak, only to shut it tight again. Frustrated with himself for the way that he had tried to hide himself away from the watchful eyes of society, he recalled hurrying into the haberdashery shop to *avoid* the young ladies who might otherwise have seen him. How had Lord Newforth known he had done such a thing? Had he been watching him? Aware of every step that Daniel had taken?

There was Lady Patience.

Triumph ran through him.

"Yes, certainly, Lord Newforth. There was one person I spoke to in particular and I am sure that they will be able to confirm that I was in town, as I have said. I certainly did *not* waste my time and my money in such a dreadful establishment as this gentleman speaks of!" He gestured to the burly fellow as he spoke, ignoring the way the man let out a low growl in response. "Though quite why I need to inform you of such a thing, I cannot understand. A gentleman's word is just as good as his bond, is it not?"

Lord Newforth only chuckled at this.

"Lord Hastings, that sounds as though you are trying to make excuses, to defend yourself and make us believe that you were doing just what you have said instead of being present in this gentleman's establishment!"

Giving Lord Newforth a small, tight-lipped smile, Daniel glanced all around him. The *ton* was listening to every word that both Daniel and Lord Newforth spoke, with many already whispering behind their fans. News would soon spread of this interaction throughout society and, were he not careful, then he would find his name covered in disgrace and shame, rather than it being held in respect. He hesitated, wondering whether or not it was right to speak Lady Patience's name in such a way. Yes, it was what he needed to do to defend himself but, at the same time, did it not mean that there might be some difficulty set upon her shoulders thereafter? Some might wonder why she had been alone in a shop with him, why no chaperones were present. There might be whispers about *her* thereafter and that was certainly not what Daniel wanted.

"Lord Hastings?" Lord Newforth's voice was loud and determined, making Daniel's lip curl. "We are all waiting to hear your defense! Baron Stillforth states that you were at his establishment yesterday afternoon, that you were with the ladies of his house and drank much of his fine brandy and the like. Thereafter, you returned home to prepare for the card party which you attended and did not pay him a single penny of what you owed."

"All of which is a lie. He must be mistaken." Daniel threw out his hands. "I have told you the truth and quite frankly, I now demand an apology from both yourself, *and* from you also, Baron Stillforth. To shame me in such a way with these despicable lies is more than a little improper and I demand that you retract your statements at once!"

"But you cannot prove it!" Lord Newforth took another step closer to Daniel, his voice seeming to echo around the room. "You say that you were in town, at only *one* shop, and that you spoke to someone there, but you cannot tell us who that was!"

"It was me."

Daniel's heart leaped up into his throat as Lady Patience emerged from the crowd, her face pink but her gaze determined.

"I was in the haberdashery shop, and can confirm that Lord Hastings was present there – and for some time also," she continued, coming to stand beside Daniel and Isabella. "The shopkeeper can confirm it also, if you wish, Lord Newforth for Lord Hastings made some purchases while he was there."

A slight smirk crossed Daniel's face as Lord Newforth's smug, confident expression changed in an instant. Instead of appearing proud and determined, he shrunk just a little, his brow furrowing and his shoulders dropping.

"You are mistaken, sir," Lady Patience continued, looking now to the Baron. "Whoever it is that gave you Lord Hastings' name must have done so to put the blame onto him, just as you are doing now." She glanced at Daniel and then back to Lord Newforth. "If you will not take my word for it, nor the word of the shopkeeper also, then you might wish to speak with my mother and my aunt, for they both saw Lord Hastings as he walked out of the shop with his purchases."

The Baron blinked, then threw a look at Lord Newforth, confirming to Daniel that the gentlemen shared a connection in some way. This had been planned and now, thanks to Lady Patience, it had shattered completely.

"Thank you, Lady Patience, for confirming that." Daniel smiled at her, then looked back to Lord Newforth, his eyebrows lifting just a little. "Now, the apology, if you please?" He turned his gaze to the Baron. "And from you also. I should like you to inform everyone listening that it is clear now that you have made a mistake, and I was *not* the one present."

The Baron gave another look to Lord Newforth, only to then shrug and drop his head. "I apologize," he muttered, his shoulders rounding now. "I must have either been deceived or made a mistake."

"Indeed. I am grateful to you for acknowledging such a thing." With a look at Lord Newforth, Daniel spread out his hands. "Whenever you are ready, Lord Newforth. I must say, I cannot understand why you appear so very determined to have such mistruths spoken about me in such a public place. I would have thought that a gentleman might seek to defend another member of the *ton*." Hearing a slight ripple of murmurings going around the gathered group, Daniel let his lips lift just a little, making it clear to Lord Newforth that, yet again, he had been defeated. Now the *ton* would be speaking of him rather than of Daniel, wondering the same questions that Daniel himself had just put to him. "The apology, Lord Newforth. I am quite deserving of it, and I will not stand to have you say nothing."

Lord Newforth stood as tall as he could, clicking his heels together and giving Daniel a somewhat superior look. Daniel lifted one eyebrow, glancing around the ballroom again for just a moment, and seeing how many present were *also* looking at Lord Newforth to see what he had to say. Waiting patiently and feeling as though even the orchestra had quietened their playing to hear Lord Newforth speak, Daniel's breath quickened as still, Lord Newforth said nothing.

And then, the gentleman sighed heavily and then inclined his head.

"My heartfelt and most sincere apologies," he said, in a tone that was nothing but regretful. "How foolish I was to believe this gentleman—" he indicated the Baron, "without so much as considering that there might have been some mistake. Forgive me." Daniel did not answer, seeing the cold glint in Lord Newforth's eyes and knowing that he did not mean a single word of what he had said. "Now, if you will excuse me," Lord Newforth continued, lifting his chin and then turning away. "I shall take my leave, I think."

The Baron did the same, scuttling away though, Daniel noticed, in the same direction as Lord Newforth. No doubt the two gentlemen would have some things to say to one another, though Daniel fully expected Lord Newforth to be utterly furious.

"Goodness."

Daniel turned his attention directly towards Lady Patience, who was watching Lord Newforth leave in much the same way as he was doing.

"Lady Patience, I do not think that I can offer you enough thanks for what you have done for me," he said, putting one hand to his heart as slowly, the crowd around them began to dissipate. "Had you not spoken as you did, then I would now find myself in a very difficult situation, I am sure."

"You should have said that it was I who had seen you in the shop." Her clear blue eyes searched his, her face a little flushed. "There was no need to hide that from anyone."

Daniel shook his head.

"I did not want to speak so, for fear that I might either upset you by speaking of such a thing without your consent or bring the *ton* to question whether or not we had been alone together in the shop."

A fire suddenly erupted in his heart as though that very

thing – to be alone with her – was precisely what he wanted more of. Lady Patience did not look away, however, though, from where he stood, it appeared that her expression softened a little.

"You are most considerate." She put one hand on his arm briefly, then pulled it away. "To consider me over yourself speaks of an excellent character, Lord Hastings."

He looked away then, a little embarrassed to be spoken about in such a way.

"It is a gentleman's duty, that is all."

When he let his gaze turn back toward hers, the softness around her eyes seemed to draw him in all the more, practically melding his eyes with hers.

"This is the second time that Lord Newforth has attempted to cause you difficulty, is it not?" Daniel frowned and Lady Patience hastily looked away, her hands now clasping in front of her. "Forgive me, I ought not to be asking such impertinent questions, but I confess that I cannot help my curiosity."

Not wishing for her to be in the least bit perturbed, not after all that she had done for him, Daniel quickly adjusted his expression and then, when she did not look at him, touched her arm gently.

"Lady Patience, you need not apologize, not when you have saved me twice from Lord Newforth!" He dropped his hand when she smiled. "But mayhap now is not the occasion to tell you all of it."

The urge to tell her the truth, to explain all that had happened, was strong indeed and he could not help but give in to that desire. There was a connection between them now, he was aware of that, though quite what he was to do with such a connection, Daniel could not say as yet.

"I understand."

The smile on her face dropped but Daniel stepped a little closer to her at once, keeping her gaze.

"Might you care for a walk through the park tomorrow?"

Surprise leaped into her face and Daniel suddenly feared that she would refuse him, that what he had asked would not be welcomed by her. Beginning to stammer, he stopped when Lady Patience's smile returned in an even greater beauty than before, relief taking hold of his heart.

"That would be lovely, Lord Hastings. I thank you."

"But of course." He swept into a bow. "Until tomorrow, then, Lady Patience. And might I thank you again for your assistance. It has changed everything for me."

Her smile sent light shining into her eyes.

"But of course, Lord Hastings. You are most welcome."

CHAPTER TWELVE

"Are you nervous?"
Patience threw a glance at Christina.
"No, I am not nervous."

That was nothing more than a lie, however, and from the way that Christina rolled her eyes, Patience knew that she did not believe her. The request from Lord Hastings to take a walk through the park so that he might explain all to her had come as something of a surprise, but a welcome surprise, all the same. Patience had been thrilled at the thought of being in his company again, seeing it as a promise that yes, he fully believed and had accepted all that she had told him about the drawing in The London Chronicle. And, at the same time, Patience had to admit a certain interest in the gentleman. The way that he had looked into her eyes as he had thanked her for what she had done – which, to her mind, had been nothing very significant – had made her heart lift and, within that, a gentle affection began to form. It had not been a feeling she had ever experienced before and yet, she had welcomed it. So, when he had asked her to take a walk in the park with him, she had nothing other than acceptance on her lips.

"There is no need for nervousness," Christina said, interrupting her thoughts. "I can see that you are a little anxious, but there is nothing to be worried about! Lord Hastings has asked to see you, and that should make you feel more than contented."

Patience nodded and looked out of the window, refusing to answer her sister's remarks. She did not want to admit to Christina that yes, she was nervous, but also that her mind was filled with thoughts and questions about what this situation with Lord Newforth might be. It was very strange that this fellow appeared to be so angry with Lord Hastings, for what possible reason could there be for a gentleman to try to shame another in such an obvious manner? Patience did not understand it and yet, she was not only glad that she had been able to aid Lord Hastings on both occasions but was also a little overcome by how willing he was to trust her with the truth.

"There he is, waiting for you."

Patience's breath hitched as her eyes fell upon Lord Hastings, seeing him smile at her as the carriage came to a slow stop. He was, she had to admit, all the more handsome this afternoon, and that made her a little flustered.

"Good afternoon, Lady Patience. Lady Christina." Lord Hastings inclined his head and then stepped forward to help them both down from the carriage, in lieu of the footman. "Thank you for joining me, Lady Patience. I must admit, I have been looking forward to our time together."

"As have I." Patience turned her head to see a second carriage coming to a stop, gesturing to it. "My mother, my aunt – Lady Pearson – and my cousin, Lady Eleanor, have come to join us. My mother wished to speak with her sister during our drive here, you understand."

A broad smile split Lord Hastings' face, making Patience blush. Did he think that her mother and Lady Pearson had been talking about him, and the walk he was to take with Patience? She could not deny that such a thing would, most likely, have been the conversation, but all the same, she did not want *him* to think such a thing though, she considered, he did not appear to be in the least bit embarrassed about it, given the way that he smiled.

How different he appears from the angry gentleman who threw such demands in my face only a few short days ago!

As though he knew what she was thinking, Lord Hastings turned to her and offered his arm.

"Shall we begin our walk, Lady Patience? And I will be able to explain to you all about what has been taking place and why I have been so... disinterested in society as a whole."

With a glance to her sister and then to her mother, who gave her a small nod, Patience accepted Lord Hastings' arm and began to walk alongside him through St James' Park. They walked in silence for a short time, though there was no nervousness or anxiety within her heart over it. She felt rather contented to be so, she realized, smiling gently to herself as the sun shone brightly overhead.

"As I said last evening, I want to thank you for what you did, in preventing Lord Newforth from bringing shame to me and my family name." Lord Hastings looked at her, then settled his free hand, upon her fingers for only a brief touch, though it was enough to convey his deep gratitude. "Yes, as you have noticed, Lord Newforth has been attempting to bring disgrace to my name and, as you witnessed at our first meeting, he is eager to cause me as much harm as he can."

He winced. "It appears that Lord Newforth is not a pleasant gentleman."

"Yes, I can see that." Patience studied Lord Hastings before saying anything more, seeing the way that his jaw tightened and his lips pulled flat. "Why does he have such a disagreement with you?" A slight tightness came into her stomach as though she ought not to be asking such a thing, but the Viscount only nodded and then, after releasing a heavy sigh, finally answered.

"If I am to tell you the truth, Lady Patience, might you promise to keep secret what I tell you? I do not ask for myself, but for the sake of another."

"But of course." Patience put as much fervency into her words as she could. "I am already honored by your willingness to share this with me, whatever it is."

The Viscount smiled again, and Patience's heart lifted all the more, thinking him so very altered in both appearance and character now. He was not dismal nor dark-tempered, but smiling and speaking words of kindness and gentleness. His manner was calm and quiet, not morose nor poor in temper. Instead, he appeared to be more contented than she had ever seen him.

"It is I who am honored, given all that you have done for me." Again, that soft, quiet smile was sent to her and Patience's heart quickened inexplicably. She could not look anywhere but his eyes, struggling to understand the emotions that suddenly swamped her. "As regards Lord Newforth, it is a sorrowful tale," the gentleman continued as Patience quietly demanded that she pay attention to everything that he said and not focus on what her thoughts and feelings were. "He came to me last Season and told me that he wished to court Isabella."

Patience's eyebrows lifted high as surprise spread out

across her chest, but she kept silent, seeing the way that Lord Hastings scowled.

"I learned about his character and, given that my mother was already most insistent that my sister have a Season to enjoy herself rather than pursue a match, I refused him. This did not make him particularly happy, especially when I was forced to go into detail as to why I would not allow him to marry her."

"I can imagine that he would not have been very pleased," Patience murmured, as a mirthless laugh escaped from Lord Hastings' lips.

"Indeed not. He was absolutely furious – I do not think that I have ever seen a gentleman so angry – and told me that I could not deny him."

Patience blinked in astonishment.

"What arrogance!" She offered him another small glance, licking her lips before she asked her question, wondering if it was a little too forward. "Might I ask what the reason was for his determination to wed her? If it is not too bold to ask."

"Not in the least." Lord Hastings shook his head. "It appears that her dowry and yearly income were all that he desired."

Closing her eyes for a moment, Patience blew out a long breath.

"You were wise to refuse him, Lord Hastings. It seems to me that he might have made your sister very miserable indeed. It is a kind, considerate gentleman who thinks of his sister's happiness in such a way."

Lord Hastings smiled but then shrugged.

"I could never have permitted her to marry such an arrogant, inconsiderate fellow."

"And that is why he pursues you in such a relentless

manner?" Patience frowned. "He wishes to shame you because you refused him Isabella's hand?"

When Lord Hastings did not immediately answer, Patience's heart slammed hard into her chest. Was there something more?

"Lord Newforth attempted to force my hand." Coming to a stop, Lord Hastings turned to face Patience directly, though her hand was still tight on his arm. "This is where I must beg for your silence over what I am to share with you, Lady Patience, for no one else knows of it." Patience nodded. Lord Hastings swallowed hard, then began to walk again though, this time, there was a good deal more slowness in his steps. "The night that my sister became betrothed to Lord Milthorpe was not a happy one, despite what you might think."

"No?"

He shook his head.

"Lord Newforth stole my sister away, forcing her into the gardens without a chaperone. Unwittingly, I was brought to find them both there and, thus, Lord Newforth demanded that my sister be given to him, as his bride."

Shock snatched away Patience's breath, one hand flying to her mouth as Lord Hastings looked into her eyes and then nodded.

"It is just as dreadful as I have said," he muttered. "Lord Newforth told me that if I did not do as he asked, then all of society would know of my sister's presence with him in the gardens and thus, her reputation would be quite ruined."

Patience shuddered.

"Oh, how dreadful."

"Lord Milthorpe offered for Isabella at that very moment," Lord Hastings continued, speaking quietly now. "I accepted and Lord Newforth's plan came to ruination.

Milthorpe then made the announcement immediately, before the entire ton, of their betrothal, so that Lord Newforth had no chance to do anything to prevent it. But had it not been for Milthorpe, then I am sure that I would not have known what to do! *That* is why Lord Newforth wishes to injure me in any way that he can, you understand."

Nodding slowly, Patience let out a sigh.

"And it is also the reason that you appear a good deal more distant from the *ton,* is it not? You recognize that the shame they can bring upon a person, even when they do not deserve it, is severe indeed." She winced. "Society can be something of a beast, sometimes." Lord Hastings looked at her, surprise sparkling in his eyes, and Patience flushed. "Did I say something wrong?"

"No, no, not at all." Lord Hastings blinked, then turned his head back so that his gaze was on the path. "It is only that you surprise me, Lady Patience. I did not think that you would be able to understand my reluctance to be a part of the *ton,* but it seems that you understand completely."

"I do." Patience smiled but then shook her head. "Though you are in a dreadful situation, Lord Hastings. Lord Newforth is a wicked man, and determined to do what he can to bring down your reputation within society, despite the fact that you have pulled back from the *ton* in such a way."

Lord Hastings shook his head.

"I care only for Isabella, not for myself."

"But if Lord Newforth succeeds, then will he not injure your sister because of what happens to *your* reputation?" When Lord Hastings turned his gaze to hers again, Patience ducked her head. "Forgive me, I do not mean to speak out of turn but–"

"You are not." Lord Hastings pressed her hand with his free one for just a moment, but he did not smile. "I suppose that he might, but my sister is soon to marry, and her reputation will then be tied to that of her husband."

"And what of yourself?"

At these words, a tiny flicker of color came into Lord Hastings' cheeks, just as Patience realized what she had said. She turned her head away directly, her heart clamoring within her chest as embarrassment ran hot from the top of her head to her toes. She had been speaking of the Viscount's prospects for marriage, without really thinking about what she was saying. Did he think that she was interested in that matter solely for herself?

"You are not the first who has made such a remark, Lady Patience." Lord Hastings cleared his throat and then smiled, though as Patience glanced back at him, she thought it a little forced. "Lord Newforth has made it quite clear to me what it is that he intends to do but, at the same time, has been entirely unspecific as to what that might be."

"And the Baron accusing you of such despicable deeds was Lord Newforth's first attempt," Patience murmured, a line forming between her eyebrows. "It appears to me, Lord Hastings, that you might require a little assistance in this situation."

Lord Hastings chuckled darkly.

"Yes, Lady Patience, I believe that I need as much help as I can find, for I am quite at a loss as to what to do to prepare for Lord Newforth's next attack upon me!"

Patience took a small breath, then set her shoulders and lifted her chin.

"Might I offer my assistance, then? I am not quite certain what I could do, but I would be glad to help you in any way I can."

"You?" Lord Hastings stopped walking again and then turned his head to look straight into her eyes as though he could not quite believe what it was that she had said. "You wish to help me, even though you have done more than enough already?"

"I do, yes." Her toes curled in her shoes as she spread out her hands. "I am not certain what it is that I could do, as I have said, but I do not think that you should face this matter alone. Lord Milthorpe and Miss Spearton will be busy planning their wedding, I suppose, and though I am sure you have other friends who can stand alongside you, I should also like to offer my help."

For some moments, Lord Hastings said nothing. Instead, he simply looked back into her face, his eyes rounding just a little as though he was slowly beginning to realize what it was that she had offered. Patience, glancing to her right and seeing her mother and aunt standing a little away from them, watching them both, felt another flush of heat flow through her. Perhaps she had been foolish to offer this, perhaps she had been a little too forward. It was not her affair to worry about and yet, all the same, her heart had yearned to do what she could to be of aid.

"My dear Lady Patience, I do not think that I have ever met a creature such as you."

Patience did not know what to make of this, seeing that either he might go on to state that she was so *very* extraordinary, he could not bring himself to be in her company any longer or to accept her offer of assistance with gratitude. To her utter relief, it was the latter.

"I am overwhelmed by your generous spirit, Lady Patience." Lord Hastings dropped Patience's hand from his arm, only to catch it with his hand and then, much to Patience's surprise, reaching for the other one also. He stood for another long moment, looking at her with a gentleness in his eyes and a soft smile on his face which made Patience's heart squeeze. "I should be grateful for anything you have to offer... so long as it does not distract you from your own activities this Season."

Patience looked away just as Lord Hastings dropped her hands from his, making to walk along the path again, though he did quickly offer her his arm.

"I am sure that I will not have any difficulty," was all she could say, not quite able to look at him. He was aware that she would be seeking out a match this Season, and his concern for her in that way again demonstrated his considerate nature. "Though what do you think we ought to do to stop Lord Newforth?"

Lord Hastings tilted his head, considering, though he did not look at her.

"I cannot be sure. At the present moment, I think that it might well be wise for me to stay often in company so that Lord Newforth cannot bring another situation to me as he did with Baron Stillforth." One eyebrow lifted just a little as he looked at her, sidelong. "Might I ask if that is something you might wish to assist me with?"

"I would, very much."

The words left her lips before Patience had a chance to truly consider her answer, her heart betraying her. She looked back at Lord Hastings all the same, however, and saw him smile just as her own lips lifted.

"Capital." Lord Hastings let out a long breath as his smile grew all the wider. "That brings me a good deal of relief, Lady Patience and, as for whatever else he might be scheming, I shall simply have to be on my guard."

"And I can be watchful," Patience suggested, as Lord Hastings nodded. "I am certain that, in time, Lord

Newforth will see that he will be nothing but unsuccessful, and will give up his pursuit of your shame."

At this, Lord Hastings' expression darkened, and he shook his head, clearly disagreeing with her.

"As much as I might wish it, Lady Patience, I cannot have the same assurance as you. I very much fear that Lord Newforth will try and try and try again until, in some way, he finds his success."

~

"What is it you are looking at?"

Patience hushed Lady Eleanor, watching Lord Newforth out of the corner of her eye.

"Hush, Eleanor. Do not draw attention to me in such a way."

Eleanor frowned.

"Patience, what is troubling you? I have never seen you so serious at any soiree before!"

"It is not the soiree but rather Lord Newforth," Patience answered, quietly, seeing Lord Newforth laughing aloud at something another gentleman had said. "I must watch him, Eleanor, that is all. He is not a good man and has, I fear, already sought to injure someone I am acquainted with."

"And by that, you mean Lord Hastings."

Patience threw a look at her cousin that said that she would not say either yes or no to that statement.

"Lord Newforth is not a gentleman to be trifled with." Eleanor's expression darkened. "He is a gentleman full of pride, with a determination to do all that he wants in whatever way he wishes. I would advise you to avoid him if you can."

"He knows my name, however," Patience answered,

quietly. "He knows that I was the one standing with Lord Hastings in the shop, making it quite clear to all that what Lord Hastings had been accused of was false. So yes, I shall do my best to avoid him, but I also must be watchful of his actions for fear that he can hurt others."

"Lady Patience?"

A young lady approached them, and Patience nodded, recognizing her face, but aware that they had not been introduced. Eleanor stepped back, clearly aware that this young lady had every intention of speaking solely to Patience.

"My brother told me about your recent conversation." Miss Spearton reached out and took Patience's hand, tears in her eyes. "Thank you for your discretion, *and* for your willingness to help us. I know that he has been carrying a heavy burden of late, though he has not told me much of it."

"But of course." Patience smiled and pressed the young lady's hand, trying to encourage her. "You must have a great deal to plan for your upcoming wedding, however! That is a wonderful thing, and very exciting too, I am sure. You must not worry too much about your brother, for that is not at all what he wants for you."

"You are most kind." Miss Spearton released Patience's hand and then took a steadying breath. "Now, I must return to my betrothed. He is waiting for me."

"But of course."

Patience watched as the lady took her leave, looking to then speak to Eleanor again, only for someone else to approach.

"Lady Patience, is it not?"

Patience nodded slowly.

"Yes, I am. Though I do not think that we are acquainted, however."

The lady smiled, lines forming around her eyes.

"We are not, but I am acquainted with your mother." She put one hand to her heart. "Lady Winters."

"Lady Winters, good evening." Patience looked at Eleanor, though her cousin had decided to stand back from this conversation also, clearly desirous not to interrupt. "I hope that you are enjoying the ball."

The lady chuckled.

"My dancing days are far behind me, Lady Patience, though my daughter, Lady Madeline, is here for the Season this year. She is soon to make a very happy match, however."

"I am very glad for her," Patience answered, throwing another glance towards Eleanor, given that she found the conversation a little awkward, but her cousin was now in deep conversation with another. "I do hope that she will be very happy."

All of a sudden, Lady Winters stepped closer to Patience, grabbed her arm, and pulled her face close.

"Listen to me, Lady Patience," she hissed, as Patience, cold with shock, could only stare into the lady's eyes. "If you draw near Lord Hastings, if you so much as *dare* to be in company with him, then it will be all the worse for you. Do you understand me?"

Patience blinked rapidly, her eyes flaring wide.

"I – I beg your pardon?"

"I have seen you in the park, at the ball, in deep conversation," the lady continued, her harsh whispers sending streaks of fright down Patience's spine. "I do not know what you mean by it, but you are to stay away from him, do you hear me?"

"I – I do not know what you mean. We are acquainted, that is all." Patience pulled herself back forcibly, yanking her arm from the older lady's grip. "I have no intention of stepping away from him."

Lady Winters glowered angrily at Patience, though Patience gazed back without flinching, although her heart was hammering furiously.

"Then you will find yourself caught up in the consequences that are soon to befall him," Lady Winters threw out at her, her face scrunched up into an expression of fury. "You have been warned, Lady Patience. And you will not be given another one."

"I think it is time for you to take your leave, Lady Winters." Patience lifted her chin and pulled her gaze away just as Eleanor came to join her. "Good evening."

Lady Winters said nothing, turning on her heel and storming away from Patience without so much as a backward look.

"Whatever was that about?" Eleanor looked at Patience, worry in her eyes. "I did not think that you were acquainted with Lady Winters."

"I am not."

Eleanor frowned.

"Then why did she come to seek you out in such a way?"

Patience shook her head, swallowing her words. It would be better not to explain all to Eleanor, for her cousin would only worry.

"It does not matter."

"You need to be careful." Eleanor clicked her tongue. "Lady Winters is aunt to Lord Newforth."

Snatching in a gasp of surprise, Paticnce closed her eyes briefly, anxiety beginning to curl in her stomach. Now, it all made sense.

"Thank you for telling me, Eleanor. I was unaware of that."

Eleanor took Patience's hand, coming around to face her with a serious expression on her face – one that was most unusual for her.

"Patience, I must ask you. Are you sure that your connection with Lord Hastings is worth this difficulty? And you need not deny it, or pretend that it is not to do with Lord Hastings, for I am very well aware that it is him that you have been speaking with. And that, somehow, there is a connection to Lord Newforth who, from what I have heard, was clearly desirous to injure him in some way."

Considering all that her friend had said, Patience hesitated for a few moments before answering.

"Yes, I am sure that it is," she said, calmly. "Lord Hastings has done nothing wrong and there is no reason for me *not* to be as connected with him as I desire to be. Lord Newforth and Lady Winters will neither frighten me nor chase me away."

Besides which, she thought silently, *I think that my heart would ache should I step away from him. Slowly but with great certainty, Lord Hastings has begun to take hold of my heart.*

CHAPTER THIRTEEN

"Have you seen the drawings in The London Chronicle?"

Daniel smiled at his mother.

"Yes, I have. I have seen every one of them, I think, for they are quite remarkable."

His mother nodded, setting the paper down.

"Is Lady Patience not the one you took tea with yesterday?"

"And the one you took a walk in the park with only a few days ago?"

Daniel turned his head just as Isabella came into the dining room.

"Yes, my dear sister, the very same."

"I did go to speak with her at the ball some two evenings ago." Isabella sat down and gratefully accepted the cup of tea from her mother. "I think that she is very pleasing."

She shared a look with their mother before turning her attention back to Daniel, who immediately began to scowl.

"Why ever do you look like that?" Lady Hastings threw up her hands. "All we are doing is enquiring about the young lady that you are spending time with, and this is the response that you give us? You think to scowl at us?"

She spoke with firmness in her voice but with a twinkle in her eye which told Daniel that she knew precisely what she was doing – and how it was making him feel.

"I think that Lady Patience is a young lady like no other," Daniel admitted, deciding to be entirely honest. "I was *most* disagreeable, I confess it, but she has been forgiving, understanding, and more than willing to spend time with me, and assist me, even though I have not asked her to do so." Again, his mother and Isabella shared a look and, a little exasperated, Daniel threw up his hands. "But that does not mean anything, of course. Might I remind you that I am concentrating solely on Isabella's wedding at this juncture?"

And seeking to avoid all that Lord Newforth might seek to do.

"Very well, very well." Lady Hastings waved one hand vaguely as Isabella giggled, turning her head away. "We shall not ask you any longer. Though, she does have something of a reputation now, given that her drawings are printed in The London Chronicle."

"A *good* reputation, yes?"

Lady Hastings nodded in answer to Daniel's question.

"Yes, of course. All of the *ton* think well of her, given her talent!"

Daniel smiled, the lady coming to the forefront of his mind.

And I want nothing whatsoever to damage that.

∽

"Hastings."

Daniel, picking up a glass of brandy, turned to his friend.

"Milthorpe, good evening."

His friend grabbed his arm, his eyes wide.

"You must leave this soiree at once."

Daniel frowned, his heart thudding suddenly.

"Why?"

"Because." Lord Milthorpe closed his eyes and took a long breath. "Because you cannot be seen here. You must go elsewhere, and be found at another event."

The frown on Daniel's face grew all the heavier.

"I do not understand."

Lord Milthorpe took another deep breath, his face white.

"Lady Winters has begun to inform everyone that you are courting her daughter. That your intention is to marry her and thus, she expects a betrothal announcement to be made very soon."

Daniel's stomach lurched.

"I beg your pardon?"

"Lady Madeline, yes." Lord Milthorpe shook his head. "I have overheard it as I came into the drawing room and came immediately to find you."

His head began to spin as Daniel fought to make sense of what he was hearing.

"I cannot understand what her intentions are."

"Except that it will not be her," Lord Milthorpe answered, coming closer to Daniel. "This must be Lord Newforth and, for whatever reason, Lady Winters has agreed to this new dark plan."

This made very little sense to Daniel but, with a nod, he threw back the glass of brandy and then made his way to the door.

"I thank you. I will do what I can to make my way from the house without being seen. I do not know the motivations of the lady but—"

"Hurry." Interrupting him, Lord Milthorpe gestured to the door. "Go, now before it is too late."

His breath hitching, Daniel scurried around the side of the drawing room and, after a momentary pause, left the room. It took him a few minutes to make his way to the front door of the house – catching a few confused glances from some of the footmen as he passed – but with relief pouring into his chest, he made his way out of the house onto the street.

Whatever is the intention here? Wondering silently to himself, Daniel quickly found his carriage, surprising the driver who quickly opened the door for Daniel before hurrying to prepare the horses. *Why would Lord Newforth and Lady Winters declare that I am courting Lady Madeline? Why would they do such a thing?*

"Where am I to go, my Lord?"

Daniel closed his eyes and leaned his head back against the squabs. Searching his mind, he eventually recalled that he had been required to decline an invitation from Lord and Lady Worthington, given that he had already accepted an invitation to this soiree.

"To Lord Worthington's townhouse," he called and, with another fresh wave of relief overpowering him, felt the carriage begin to rock gently as it pulled away from the house. Yes, he had made his escape, but the difficulties still remained. Lord Newforth had plans to do whatever he could to bring what he considered to be consequences down upon Daniel and, with growing concern, Daniel realized that the fellow might never stop until he had succeeded. Just what was he to do? How could he put an end to Lord Newforth's intentions and protect himself at the same time?

The carriage soon came to a stop and, his questions still unanswered, Daniel stepped down and hurried into the townhouse. The ball was already well underway, and no one saw him step inside - no one save for a few footmen. Letting out a slow breath, a trickle of sweat running down his back, Daniel picked up a glass from the table and sipped it, hoping that no one would see that he was flustered and upset.

"Lord Hastings, good evening."

A flood of happiness ran through him as Lady Patience came to speak with him, her eyes and expression gentle.

"Lady Patience." He inclined his head. "I am very glad to see you." Seeing her eyes flare suddenly, he flushed hot and then tried to explain. "I have come from a soiree, one where I had intended to remain, but Lord Milthorpe gave me a warning and thus, I had to rush from that to this!"

"A warning?" Lady Patience's hand caught his for just a moment. "What has happened?"

Daniel swallowed, the heat in his face only growing as he explained.

"Lord Milthorpe overheard Lady Winters informing those present that I am now courting her daughter, Lady Madeline. I do not know why she seeks to do such a thing, and mayhap you will not understand given that you are unaware of her connection to Lord Newforth but–"

"She is his aunt, yes?" Lady Patience smiled tightly. "She came to warn me to stay away from you, Lord Hastings."

A strand of fear wrapped around Daniel's heart.

"When did she say this?"

"Recently." Lady Patience shrugged lightly. "Not that I

have any intention of listening to a word that she says, of course."

Daniel swallowed, hard.

"I think that you must be careful, Lady Patience. When it comes to Lady Winters and Lord Newforth, there is severe danger there. If she has come to warn you, then it will be because you have been noticed by him. You should stay away from me."

"I can make such a decision for myself, and I am not about to be intimidated into changing my mind on what I have already decided." She tossed her head, her eyes flashing suddenly. "I do not appreciate what was said to me."

Admiration rose like a fountain in Daniel's chest as he gazed at her, his struggles seeming now to fade away.

"So long as you are sure, Lady Patience."

"I am." Her smile returned, though it disappeared shortly thereafter. "Why, do you think, did Lady Winters do such a thing? Why would she push her daughter into such a connection when it is false?"

Daniel shook his head.

"I do not know. But I did as Lord Milthorpe suggested and made my way from the soiree just as soon as I could."

Lady Patience's eyes suddenly rounded.

"What if she intends to use her daughter to bring shame to you? What if they have decided to work together to make the *ton* turn against you? She declares that you are courting Lady Madeline and that she expects a betrothal very soon – and what choice is left for you but to deny it? You will say that you are *not* courting the lady, that you have no intention of offering for her hand and, thereafter, Lady Winters will declare her daughter to be utterly heartbroken, telling us all that you have been both ungentlemanly and cruel."

A cold sweat broke out across Daniel's forehead as he saw the truth in Lady Patience's suggestions.

"What is worse, she might declare that I have treated Lady Madeline in a... less than suitable manner." He closed his eyes, wincing. "Lady Winters could say anything she wishes, and the *ton* will, no doubt, believe her, for, if the injured party is a young lady, then they are inclined to trust *her*." He ran one hand through his hair, panic gripping him. "What am I to do?"

Lady Patience took his hand again, squeezing it gently until he looked at her. Her smile wobbled a little, and there was hesitancy in her voice as she spoke.

"Then, Lord Hastings, the only thing you can do is pre-empt her."

He blinked, confused.

"You must declare yourself to be courting another young lady – and you must do so now," Lady Patience continued, her voice hitching as her hand trembled lightly in his. "That way, Lady Winters will appear to be either confused or deceitful, seeking to push her daughter into your path, rather than accepting the news that you are courting another."

Daniel's throat constricted.

"All the same, if I am only courting someone, she might then state that I ended my courtship of Lady Madeline to pursue another – and could, also, state that I had been cruel and demeaning to Lady Madeline beforehand." Rubbing one hand over his eyes, his chest tightened as he forced himself to look into Lady Patience's eyes. "I would have to declare myself betrothed." A silence followed his statement and Daniel withered inwardly, his gaze tugging away from her. He had asked too much of her, even though he had not been explicit in his words. It was clear to him that she understood what he meant by such a statement, given the pink now in her cheeks but, as the quiet grew, Daniel dropped his head to his chest. "This is not your concern, Lady Patience." Mumbling now, he shook his head to himself. "I will find another way, I will–"

"I would accept if you asked it of me."

Daniel's head lifted sharply, astonishment catching him.

"It is not the way that matches are usually made, I know, but if this will save you then I will accept." Lady Patience's gaze was steady, though her fingers twisted together in front of her. "It will come as a surprise to my family, but they will not object. You have fortune enough to satisfy them."

This was said with a wry smile, and Daniel's heart squeezed painfully. He was aware of just what it was that she was offering him – and how much their lives might change if he moved forward with it – and took lots of small, sharp breaths as he came to understand what would happen should he do this.

"I can end our betrothal later, should you wish to make your own choice," he said, a trifle hoarsely, coughing to clear his throat. "I will take the blame, should you decide such a thing. I understand how significant this will be, and I do not want to force you to do this. You have said that you will aid me in my difficulties with Lord Newforth, for which I am very grateful, but nor do I want you to give up your freedom because of me. That is not required."

She tilted her head just a little.

"And what if I wish to?" Daniel lowered his head, overcome. He had found such a jewel in Lady Patience's company and in recognizing that, he felt himself utterly unworthy. "If you realize now that you do not want to pursue this, however, then I understand."

"No, it is not that." Lifting his head, Daniel looked into Lady Patience's eyes and then, seeing her hand still in his, set his other one atop their joined hands. "It is because I feel myself to be so unworthy of you, Lady Patience. We have only just begun our acquaintance, and yet I have found a true friend in you. You are selfless, considerate, and with a kinder heart within you than I have ever met in anyone else. So, while I am willing to make this announcement and to step forward into society with you as my betrothed, know that my heart is aware of just how great a gift I am being offered – and how much I will cherish it."

Lady Patience's eyes glistened, though she smiled with it, making him want to pull her tight against his heart. He did not, however, and they remained standing quietly again for only a few moments.

Then, Lady Patience took a breath.

"Then shall we go?" she asked, a slight tremor in her voice. "Perhaps to my mother, first?"

Daniel nodded, setting her hand on his arm, and ignoring the ball of nervousness and doubt which coiled within him, made his way into the crowd, ready to declare himself betrothed to Lady Patience.

CHAPTER FOURTEEN

"Mama?"

Patience's whole body was trembling, such was the suddenness of her new betrothal. She did not know what her mother would say to such a thing, but she was already certain that there would be no serious complaint. Yes, there would be a degree of surprise, but Lord Hastings had enough of a fortune and good standing in society for this to be nothing but accepted.

"Yes, my dear?" Lady Osterley turned, only to look up in surprise at Lord Hastings. "Oh, good evening, Lord Hastings. How very good to see you."

She smiled but then glanced down at Patience's hand on Lord Hastings' arm before turning enquiring eyes towards Patience.

"Mama, I have something to tell you." Her heart beating furiously, Patience looked back at her mother steadily, just as Christina came to join them. "Lord Hastings has asked for my hand, and I have accepted him – this in lieu of father's acceptance, of course, which I am sure will be given."

Fixing a smile on her face as she waited for her mother's response, Patience took in the astonishment that filled her mother's expression. Her eyes flared wide, her mouth rounding into a circle while Christina let out a choked sound, making Patience wince just a little.

"Betrothed?" her mother whispered, her gaze going from Patience to Lord Hastings and back again. "You wish to marry my Patience?"

Lord Hastings nodded.

"I do. Very much. My heart desires only her."

The sincerity in his tone made Patience's heart warm, only for her to close her eyes for a moment, recalling what it was that had made this betrothal take place. Lord Hastings was very kind to speak so, but there was no real truth to it, she knew. *Not as yet.* Taking a breath, she kept her smile fixed in place. Perhaps things would change, in time.

"My goodness." Lady Osterley paused for a moment, only for her then to fling her arms around Patience's neck, exclaiming wildly as she did so. "This is quite wonderful! How delightful to hear this news! I cannot believe that you have found so excellent a match, Patience, and without even an official courtship first!" Releasing her, she then grasped Lord Hastings' hand. "I know that you have been spending time in Patience's company, of course, but I did not think that such a desire would grow so quickly!"

"Well, it has." Lord Hastings beamed with what, to everyone else, looked like genuine delight, though Patience knew otherwise. "I do hope that you will permit me to tell my friends here this evening? It is wonderful news, and I should very much like to share it. Though, if you think it best to wait for Lord Osterley's consent, then I quite understand."

Lady Osterley shook her head.

"No, no, we need not wait. He will be *more* than delighted, I assure you. Of *course,* you must go and tell as many others as you wish – and I shall too."

"How wonderful." Christina stepped forward and immediately embraced Patience, though Patience caught the look of confusion that lingered in her eyes when she pulled back. "You will have to tell me all about it in greater detail later this evening, Patience. I must know how it is that Lord Hastings proposed."

"I shall." Seeing that her sister suspected that there was something more to this, Patience could only look away, turning her gaze up to Lord Hastings. "Might we take a turn about the room? I cannot recall if Eleanor is present this evening, but if she is, I should like to see her."

He nodded, his smile still in place.

"Of course." With a nod to Lady Osterley, he led them both away and Patience walked with him, feeling the need to lean into him a little more. They walked in silence for a few minutes, nodding and smiling at a few other guests, until finally, Lord Hastings spoke. "I cannot quite believe that we are betrothed." He looked down at her, his blue eyes seeming to glow with a sense of happiness, though Patience was rather surprised to see it. "I shall have to tell my mother and sister as soon as I return home. Neither of them went out this evening, for they were both a little fatigued still from a ball last evening." A slight glint came into his eyes. "We shall have to make sure that Isabella is wed first, however, since she was betrothed first."

The thought of standing up in church and making her vows to Lord Hastings sent both a flurry of pleasure and doubt running through Patience's frame. It had all been so sudden, she was still trying to take in her new situation though the fact that Lord Hastings appeared to be so contented with their betrothal did bring her a good deal of relief.

"Betrothed?"

Patience swallowed at the tightness in her throat just as Lord Hastings greeted Lady Gregson, one of the most renowned gossips in the *ton*. She had overheard Lord Hastings saying something about the betrothal and, without hesitation, had broken into their conversation to find out what it might be about. Normally, Patience might have found herself a little disinclined towards the lady's company but now, in this circumstance, she welcomed it.

"Good evening, Lady Gregson." She glanced up at Lord Hastings. "Yes, it is as you heard. Lord Hastings and I are now announcing our betrothal to the *ton*."

Lady Gregson gasped, one hand at her mouth, her eyes flaring wide as the attention of many others was caught by her actions.

"Did you say... betrothed?" Lady Gregson whispered, a small smile tipping up one side of her mouth, clearly delighted that *she* was to be the first one to know of it. "Truly?"

Lord Hastings nodded.

"Yes, we are betrothed. I wanted to wait for a little longer before telling the *ton* of my happiness, given that my sister has not even had her betrothal ball as yet but, truth be told, I could not help it! I am much too happy to keep my joy within."

Lady Gregson's eyes widened all the more.

"You mean to say that you have been betrothed for some time? Oh, Lord Hastings! How considerate of you! And Lady Patience, how patient you have been!"

Patience opened her mouth to correct the lady, but Lord Hastings set one hand on hers as it sat on his arm, quietening her. It was, she realized, a benefit to them if Lady Gregson believed that they had been betrothed for some time. That story would be spread and, therefore, anything that Lady Winters might say would be blown into fine dust, soon to be forgotten.

"I am sure that you have many a person you wish to tell," Lady Gregson continued, making to step away from them both. "I will not hold you back."

Murmuring his thanks, Lord Hastings sent a twinkling look towards Patience, a tiny smile curling one side of his lip which, seeing it, made Patience smile broadly. It was quite obvious to them both that Lady Gregson did not care about either of them but was eagerly hurrying away so that *she* might spread their news.

"For once, I find myself grateful for the *ton* and their delight in spreading whispers," Lord Hastings said, out of the corner of his mouth. "I cannot express my gratitude to you enough in this, Lady Patience." Turning his head to look straight into her eyes, his smile became a little more gentle, almost tender. "We are betrothed. And soon, all of society shall know it."

∽

"You are betrothed?" Patience rose to her feet, crossed the drawing room, and pulled her cousin into a tight hug. She said nothing, a lump in her throat as Eleanor leaned back to look into Patience's eyes, concern lingering there. "Are you happy in your betrothal?"

Patience nodded, releasing Eleanor but catching her hands instead.

"I wanted to tell you last evening, but I could not."

"That is because I was not present," Eleanor told her. "I

was at a soiree, only to hear Lady Winters make the most extraordinary statement! She informed us all that Lord Hastings was courting Lady Madeline! And that he wanted very much to betroth himself to her!"

Licking her lips, Patience nodded.

"Eleanor, it is because of that statement that I find myself betrothed to Lord Hastings." Quickly explaining, she made her way across the room to sit back down, her cousin coming to sit beside her. "Might I ask when you heard the news?"

Eleanor smiled, a tiny gleam in her eye.

"It was at the soiree. Someone who had been at the ball came to play cards and, as he sat down, told Lord Johnstone that Lord Hastings had just declared his betrothal to Lady Patience – and not only that, that you had been betrothed for some time but had not told anyone to give Miss Spearton her happiness."

Awash with relief, Patience's shoulders dropped just a little.

"That is good. I am glad that Lady Winters' story was prevented from spreading."

Eleanor set one hand over Patience's.

"Not only that, but those at the soiree, once they had heard the news, then began to question Lady Winters as to why she would say such a thing about a gentleman who had already announced himself betrothed. Lady Winters began to stammer some explanation but another lady – I believe it was Lady Berridale – stated that she had *never* seen Lady Madeline and Lord Hastings in company, and accused Lady Winters of fabricating the connection to push her daughter a little more into society's view." She pressed Patience's hand. "I, of course, pretended that I had known about it for a long time, and had been told to remain silent.

Given what you have explained to me, I think that you and Lord Hastings have succeeded in thwarting Lord Newforth's efforts. Lady Winters is the one embarrassed and ashamed, I am afraid, though that is entirely her own doing."

Patience nodded.

"Yes, it is."

"Tell me." Eleanor lifted her hand and then tipped her head, studying Patience's face. "Are you happy with this betrothal? You have not long known Lord Hastings and I must wonder if this is a wise idea."

Patience looked down at her hands as they rested in her lap, wondering if she ought to be truthful with her cousin or if she ought to pretend that all was well, regardless of what she felt inwardly. After a few moments of quiet, she lifted her gaze back to Eleanor, then spread out her hands.

"I will admit that I have found myself a little drawn to Lord Hastings of late. We started off rather badly but that has improved significantly to the point that I have found myself eager to be in conversation with him whenever I can. I think him *very* handsome and, truth be told, when he made the suggestion that we become betrothed, there was something within my heart that flew to the skies in delight."

Eleanor's eyes continued to search Patience's face though, after another short while, she smiled.

"Then might I wish you every happiness, Patience. Though," she continued, a frown marring her otherwise warm expression, "I think that now, you must be even more on your guard. Lord Newforth will be greatly displeased, and now Lady Winters will be upset and angry also. I do not know what they will do, but I fear that they will attempt to shame you *both* in some way."

Patience pressed her lips tight together as she considered this, only to nod.

"Yes, I can see why you might be concerned, but I have made my decision. I am now betrothed to be married to Lord Hastings, and I will continue to aid him in whatever way I can against Lord Newforth."

Eleanor sighed gently but then smiled.

"You are always sure of what you want to do, are you not? I am glad for you, truly. Though, I do hope that you will continue to put your drawings into The London Chronicle? I note that *my* likeness has not yet been published within it!" She laughed as Patience giggled, her eyes twinkling. "Your work is well known in society now, Patience. You cannot give it up just because you are betrothed and now have a wedding to plan!"

Patience laughed with her cousin, her heart filled with a surge of happiness.

"I shall not stop, I assure you," she said, rising to ring the bell. "In fact, I promise you that you shall be the very next drawing I send to The London Chronicle. Will that satisfy you?"

Her cousin grinned.

"I shall be more than contented with that. Thank you, Patience."

CHAPTER FIFTEEN

"You really are quite remarkable, Lady Patience."

Daniel smiled to himself as his sister expressed yet more delight over Lady Patience's artwork.

"I recognized Lady Eleanor at once," his mother said, as both families continued to enjoy their dinner together. "I am sure that she might have been overjoyed to see her likeness in The London Chronicle!"

Lady Patience, her cheeks a little flushed, let out a soft laugh.

"I think that she is, yes, given that she practically demanded that I make *her* the very next subject of my drawings."

This brought a smile to everyone's face, and Daniel settled back into his chair a little more, thinking to himself that this dinner had been a great success. A sennight after their betrothal, he had succeeded in bringing both families together, with Lord Milthorpe joining them also. It had only added to his delight to hear that Lord Osterley had given his consent by letter, which meant that his marriage to Lady Patience could now go ahead without any difficulty.

I think that I am as delighted as any gentleman might be to find himself betrothed. Considering Lady Patience, his chest flooded with a fresh warmth as he took her in. The light smile on her lips, the sweetness of her manner, and the way that her eyes constantly turned to his made Daniel's heart lift. It had been a little over a sennight now since their unexpected betrothal, and with every day that had passed, he had found himself all the happier about their upcoming wedding.

Which is very strange indeed, given that it was not something that I had considered before then.

"Hastings?"

Pulling himself out of his thoughts – and his gaze away from Lady Patience - Daniel flushed hot as his mother's knowing look.

"Yes, Mother?"

"I think that we shall take our tea in the drawing room now." She smiled and then rose from the table, the other ladies following suit. "Do not be too long with your port. I am sure that your betrothed will be eager for your company, and you for hers!"

This was said with a twinkle in her eye and Daniel only nodded, suddenly unable to look anywhere but straight ahead. The ladies made their way from the room and, as the door closed, Lord Milthorpe immediately began to chuckle.

"They are clearly aware – as I am – that your admiration for Lady Patience grows with every moment that you spend with her."

Lord Milthorpe laughed aloud this time, as Daniel threw him what was an attempt at a withering look, though he knew all too well that what his friend had said was quite true.

"Shall we drink our port?" Gesturing to the footman to serve the port, Daniel said nothing more until a glass had been served both to himself and Lord Milthorpe. Thereafter, he raised the glass high, managing to smile. "To happy and contented marriages."

"Indeed." After drinking his glass of port, Lord Milthorpe smiled broadly. "Did I tell you that Lord Newforth has been seen in Bath?"

Daniel's eyebrows lifted in surprise.

"Has he, indeed?"

"Yes, he has. I heard it from Lord Tillerson, who has only just arrived from Bath. It may be that you have succeeded in besting him."

A slight scowl pulled at Daniel's expression.

"I do not think that betrothing myself to Lady Patience could be considered *besting* him."

"That is not what I meant." Lord Milthorpe cleared his throat. "What I am trying to say is that you may well now be free of the difficulties which have pursued you ever since my betrothal to Isabella, and can now focus on the happiness before you. Happiness which, I think, you are only just beginning to realize the extent of."

At this, Daniel looked away, trying to sort out his emotions into an easily understood collection. When it came to Lady Patience, his feelings were beginning to grow in a most confusing manner, spreading right through him until he struggled to even think of anything other than her, and when he might see her again.

"You are unsure of your feelings, mayhap?" Lord Milthorpe chuckled again though this time, it was softer. "I can well understand that."

"You can?" Daniel's eyebrows lifted as Lord Milthorpe nodded. "Then you mean to say that—"

"Yes, yes, I think that I am falling in love with Isabella." Lord Milthorpe reached to pour himself another glass of port rather than looking back at Daniel. "It has been a very strange thing, I must say. I have known Isabella for a very long time, and never once thought of her with any sort of fondness beyond friendship... and yet, here I am now, discovering that my heart holds a great affection for her! I wake in the morning wondering when I am to see her again. My eagerness and anticipation for our forthcoming wedding fills me in greater strength every day, and when I take her into my arms, I have no desire to be anywhere other than there, to linger in that moment for as long as I can."

Daniel scrubbed one hand over his face, not quite sure what to say. It was not that he felt in any way uncomfortable about what Lord Milthorpe was saying. It was more that he could recognize everything that was being said and, if he accepted it, then that meant that something almost unimaginable was happening to him.

"Might I be so bold as to ask you whether or not you have held Lady Patience close?"

A slight lift of Lord Milthorpe's eyebrows made Daniel's lips quirk ruefully as he shook his head.

"No, not as yet. Though we have danced the waltz together already... though that was when I was deeply angry and upset and had the sole intention of telling her just how I felt."

Lord Milthorpe grinned.

"Then might I suggest that you try doing so very soon? You may find yourself surprised with all that you feel – or it may bring you to a determined conclusion about what is already within your heart."

Daniel said nothing, swirling his port around the glass gently as he considered all that Lord Milthorpe had said. He was truly delighted to know that Milthorpe felt so strongly for Isabella, for that meant that, despite the difficulties with which the betrothal had begun, her future would now be settled and happy.

And can I hope for the same with my own marriage? He swallowed as a sudden thought came to him. *What if she decides to separate from me before we marry? I did give her that choice.*

"Is there something the matter?"

With a small sigh, Daniel spread out his free hand.

"I have told Lady Patience that if she wishes to end the betrothal, if she wishes to make her own match, then she has every right to do so – and that I will take the blame for the ending of it." Daniel lifted his shoulders and then let them drop. "I confess that there is a part of me that fears that she will do so and thus, all that I feel will break apart and injure me in the process."

Lord Milthorpe shrugged.

"Did she give you any indication that she planned to do such a thing?"

Daniel shook his head no.

"Then why are you concerned?"

"Because I have not felt such feelings before," Daniel admitted, his face flushing. "This was never meant to happen. I intended to step away from society once my sister was wed and now, I have found myself the center of attention thanks to my sudden and somewhat surprising betrothal! Lady Patience came unexpectedly into my sphere, but now that she has become almost a permanent part of it..." Daniel shook his head, a sudden pain in his chest. "The truth is, I cannot think of what it would be like without her."

Lord Milthorpe nodded in evident understanding.

"Then you must tell her," he said, quietly. "Take her in your arms, tell her of your heart, and you will see and feel true joy in that moment. I am quite sure of it."

∽

"Patience, wait a moment."

Daniel's heart was thudding painfully as he caught Lady Patience's hand, pulling her back from the door. Her family was about to take their leave, and in stealing her back from them as he had done, he was giving them a few moments to be alone. The surprise on her face told him that she certainly had not been expecting him to do such a thing and that almost made Daniel pull back from what he had thought to do, only for her fingers to tighten gently on his.

"Lord Milthorpe." Feeling as though his tongue was sticking to the roof of his mouth, Daniel shook his head, looked away from her, and tried again. It seemed easier to speak when he was not looking at her. "Lord Milthorpe has informed me that Lord Newforth has been seen in Bath. It may be that he has taken his leave of London and will not return."

He heard her catch her breath in a quiet gasp, his gaze going back to her.

"Can it be true?"

With a small smile, Daniel nodded.

"I think it must be. I have not heard anything as regards Lady Winters and her daughter - however, I presume that they are both still in London."

"But not seen in society very much," Lady Patience

added, her eyes glowing with clear happiness. "How wonderful for you, Hastings! You are free now of the threats he placed upon you."

"So it would seem."

A tension began to hum through him as Lord Milthorpe's advice began to ring around his mind. Would he dare to take Lady Patience in his arms? Would he be bold enough to hold her close and hope that her response would be a positive one? Or would her hand in his be all that he was left with?

"Is there something more?"

Daniel, realizing that he had been gazing at her without saying a word, nodded quickly.

"Yes, there is. It is to say that... well, I recognize that I – no, that is to say, I *recall* that I said you could – or I could – end the betrothal if you wished to be free to make your own choice." Heat seared his very bones, making him shift about from foot to foot. "If Lord Newforth has given up and made his way to Bath and if Lady Winters now appears too ashamed by what *she* has done to make any trouble, then I cannot see any reason for our betrothal to continue if you do not wish it."

A strange look came into Lady Patience's eyes. They were sharp, searching through his expression bit by bit as though she could not understand what he had said. Her lips were pressed tight together, a pinprick of color in her otherwise pale cheeks.

And then, moisture filled them.

Fear raced up Daniel's spine and into his heart.

"I did not mean to upset you, Patience!" Grasping both of her hands, he stepped closer, his words fervent. "Forgive me, I did not mean to upset you in the *least*. The only thing I meant to suggest was that you might wish to be freed from me and that I am willing to give you that freedom if you desire it."

"But I already told you." Patience was blinking quickly now, a catch in her voice. "I told you during the first conversation we had about our prospective betrothal. I said that to enter into this betrothal was what I wanted, what I wished to do. I have never mentioned stepping back from it, that was only *your* thought rather than mine."

Daniel's breathing grew a little quicker as he looked into her eyes, hating the tears that he saw there.

"I did not mean to bring you any sort of sorrow, Patience, truly. I do not want you to be upset by what I have said, I only wanted to be assured that this was truly what you wanted."

Lady Patience's lips curved for only a moment as she came all the closer, barely even an inch between them.

"Then be assured, Lord Hastings. To be wed to you is exactly what I want. In fact, I believe that I want it even more than I did when you first suggested it."

I cannot take my eyes off her.

It was as if he could no longer breathe, the gentleness of her eyes, the curve of her lips, and the sweetness of her nearness wrapping around him, tugging him closer, urging him in all the more. Daniel blinked once, twice, and then began to lower his head, seeing her eyes fluttering closed.

This is exactly what I wanted.

Their kiss was light, soft, and filled with a tenderness that spoke of Daniel's heart. It did not last overly long, but nor was it so short that it left him hungry for more. Instead, when he drew back, it was with wonder and contentment twining together through him, making him see that all he felt, all that was in his heart, spoke of a deep and growing affection that gave him the smallest taste of love.

"Patience?"

Daniel dropped Lady Patience's hand and staggered back, just as the door opened and Lady Christina peeked in, glancing at him first before looking at her sister.

"Forgive me for the interruption, but the carriage is waiting."

Her smile was knowing, and Daniel flushed hot, though he clasped his hands behind his back and kept his expression as nonchalant as he could.

"But of course. I was only telling your sister some news which was recently shared with me. Some *good* news."

Lady Patience, her eyes filled with stars, gazed back at him as her sister disappeared back through the door, expecting her to follow.

"Yes indeed, Lord Hastings. It was, I must say, very good indeed."

CHAPTER SIXTEEN

I am in love with him.
Patience lay back on the couch, one arm flung over her eyes as she let her thoughts wind around Lord Hastings and all that they had shared recently. These last ten days had brought her a flurry of emotion, every time that she had been in his company. When he had kissed her after the dinner last week, she had felt her heart fill with a fiery, new affection that had not let her go since that moment. Everything seemed to have become remarkably calm now, for the news that Lord Newforth had made his way to Bath had spread through London, and Lady Winters nor her daughter had not been seen in London for some days. Patience's betrothal to Lord Hastings appeared to have made all of their threats fade away and now, all that was left was happiness.

A quiet knock at the door interrupted Patience's thoughts and, sitting up, she permitted entry to the footman. He came in directly and handed her a letter that had only just been delivered, and Patience broke the seal and unfolded it.

'My dear Patience,' she read. *'I am in such a fluster! Miss Spearton's betrothal ball is this evening, and I have just torn my new gown! Will you come to the modiste's with me to see if she has something else I might purchase that will not require much alteration?'*

With a small sigh and shake of her head, Patience rose to her feet.

"Will you inform my sister that I have gone to see Lady Eleanor?" she said, as the footman nodded. "And have my maid ready herself at once, for I shall need to take a hackney."

Her mother had already stepped out for the morning, going to take tea with an old acquaintance, leaving Patience and Christina still at home. Christina had not even risen to break her fast as yet, and Patience knew that her mother would not mind in the least if she went to visit Eleanor for a time. She would need to return in time for dinner and, thereafter, the preparations for Miss Spearton and Lord Milthorpe's betrothal ball, but that was many hours away. Making her way to the front of the house, Patience quickly pulled on her bonnet, leaving the ribbons loose and, her maid at the ready, stepped outside. A hackney was quickly found and, after stepping inside, as her maid gave the jarvey the instructions on where they wished to go, Patience settled back as best she could, wondering whether or not she would be able to convince Eleanor that she had no need for a new gown, and that it could be repaired instead. Though, she considered, her lips twisting for a moment, that would entirely depend on just how bad the tear to the gown was, and *where* it was also.

"My Lady?"

Patience, having been lost in her contemplations, turned her head to see her maid frowning.

"Yes?"

"I don't know where we are going, but I am quite sure that this isn't the road we want to take."

A surge of uncertainty tugged at Patience's stomach.

"Mayhap the jarvey has been forced to take a different road," she suggested, trying to ignore the worry that ran through her. "There might have been some reason for his choice of path."

"Except that we are going in the opposite direction," the maid replied, her eyes rounding. "Lady Patience, I don't mean to question you, but it seems to me as though he isn't taking you where you want to go."

Patience turned her gaze to the window, the streets now unfamiliar. Her hand pressed to her stomach as she fought against the dread which filled her. Surely the driver was not deliberately taking her the wrong way? Mayhap he was mistaken or confused or...

Or mayhap Lord Newforth is not as gone from London as we were led to believe.

Fear made her stomach lurch, and Patience gripped the edge of her seat with both hands, trying to think of what to do. Could the hackney have been waiting for her to step in? But if he had been, how would he have known that she would be making her way from the house and that her mother had already taken the carriage?

Unless he has been watching me?

She closed her eyes and shuddered.

"My Lady?" The maid's voice was high-pitched, and her eyes filled with concern. "Where are we going?"

"Listen to me." Leaning forward, Patience caught the maid's hand, looking into her eyes as a steadiness burst through her, despite the fear in her veins. "When the hackney comes to a stop, you must run."

"Run?" The maid shook her head. "I can't leave you, I must–"

"You will go out through this door," Patience interrupted, gesturing to the one on her left. "I will remain by the window on the right. Once you set foot outside, you must run as fast as you can away from the hackney. Do all that you can to avoid being seen or noticed by the jarvey... or by whoever else is waiting for me."

"Waiting for you?" The maid had now gone very pale indeed. "I don't understand."

"You must go to Lord Hastings' townhouse at once and tell him where the hackney took me," Patience continued, grasping the maid's arm with her other hand, trying to keep her calm enough to listen. "Do you understand what I am asking you to do? You will not be punished or berated for leaving me behind, I assure you. If you want to keep me safe, then this is what you *must* do." Slowly, the maid began to nod, just as the hackney began to slow. Patience released her, swallowing hard against the fear that once more rose within her. "You recall what you must do?"

Again, the maid nodded, edging closer to the other side of the hackney.

"Run from here, go directly to Lord Hastings' and tell him where the hackney took you."

"Here." Patience pushed her purse into the maid's hands. "Use all that you require to get you to Lord Hastings. Do not delay. He *must* come to find me."

The maid squeezed her eyes closed and dragged in a long, ragged breath just as the hackney came to a slow stop – and Patience flung one arm out towards the maid.

"Go! Now!"

With a startled squeak, the maid threw open the door and escaped from the hackney, only for the Patience's door to open – and none other than Lord Newforth to smile up at her. The darkness in his eyes made her shudder.

"I think it would be best, Lady Patience, if you could step out of the hackney."

Patience drew herself up as tall as she could whilst, at the same time, holding onto the edge of her seat with both hands.

"I do not think that I shall, Lord Newforth. I do not know what it is that you have done in arranging to get me here, but I have no intention of stepping out of the hackney for you."

Lord Newforth smiled and the trembling in Patience's frame returned.

"Then if you do not, Lady Patience, I shall be forced to remove you myself. It is not as though the jarvey is going to make his way from this place at your request now, is it? As you can see, I have been able to ask him to do what *I* wish, and it will only be at my command that he will drive the hackney away."

Patience shook her head.

"I will not." Whatever it was that Lord Newforth intended to do, Patience did not know, but she was certainly not about to go with him willingly. "Might you explain to me what it is that you are doing, Lord Newforth? Last I heard, you were in Bath."

He chuckled, leaning forward into the space of the hackney door as Patience tried to stay exactly where she was, in an attempt to convey strength though, inwardly, fear was screaming through her.

"Ah, Lady Patience, I see that the rumors I circulated have spread and spread well! Society has its uses, does it not?" He tilted his head, watching her with hawk-like eyes, making her feel as though she was the unwilling prey, waiting for the moment he would sink his claws into her skin. "Now, you will come out of the hackney and—"

"What is it that you intend?"

Patience interrupted him, her voice shaking, only for the wicked smile to fade from Lord Newforth's face. Instead of answering, he reached out one hand, grabbed her arm, and hauled her out of the hackney. The scream stuck in her throat, her hands flailing only for pain to strike through her as Lord Newforth slammed her back bodily against the carriage, his face now close to hers, his face pulled into an ugly expression.

"I warned you to stay away from Lord Hastings, did I not?" he hissed, his eyes like sharp knives. "Lady Winters spoke to you, and yet you persisted! You have no one to blame for this but yourself, Lady Patience. This supposed betrothal is nothing but a pretense, set in place to prevent me from doing what I had to, to punish Lord Hastings. Before that, you insisted that you had been in company with him, so that the Baron's accusations fell to the dirt! You appear to be quite determined to persist with assisting Lord Hastings in this matter and thus, unfortunately, I have decided to make certain that *you* are the one who will cause Lord Hastings the greatest suffering... and the heaviest weight of shame."

Patience could not breathe, her chest painful as her lungs screamed for air. Her eyes were filled with nothing but Lord Newforth, hardly daring to imagine what it was he might be intending for her.

"You have much too great a strength in you, Lady Patience," Lord Newforth finished, finally stepping back and releasing her just a little, though not enough for her to step away. "But that does not mean that it cannot be broken."

Closing her eyes, Patience finally dragged in a breath, trying to find some of the strength that Lord Newforth had just spoken of. Whatever it was that he intended, it was clear to her that her entire future, her entire life, might well be completely and utterly ruined. She was without a chaperone, without family or anyone who could assist her, and with Lord Newforth's evil determination pulling her in whatever direction he wanted, she felt completely helpless.

"This way, Lady Patience." Stepping away, Lord Newforth pulled her with him, the streets seeming to close in around her. This was, to her, an unfamiliar part of London, a place where no one would come to look for her, where no one would recognize her, but that did not bring her any relief. Lord Newforth could do any number of things, and her reputation would be gone in a moment – and Lord Hastings' world be turned upside down. Lord Milthorpe and Miss Spearton's happiness would be shattered. It was the same sort of situation that Lord Newforth had tried to push upon Miss Spearton, where he had attempted to use society and its inclination toward gossip to get what he wanted. Now, he would do the same to her, though this time there did not appear to be any way to escape. "This little room will do," Lord Newforth muttered, pushing her through a front door and then into a room to her left. "I am afraid that this will be your home for the next few days, Lady Patience."

"My home?" Patience wrenched her arm away from him, turning to face him as he blocked the door. "What do you mean?"

Lord Newforth shrugged.

"It is just as I have said. You will not go anywhere, Lady Patience, until the rumors about your absence have washed through all of society. They will say a great many things about you, I am sure, for you are *very* well known now, given your drawings in The London Chronicle, as well as your betrothal to Lord Hastings."

Patience said nothing, though her heart was pounding furiously in her chest, and her mind fighting to find some way out of her current predicament, though she could think of none. It was not as though she could merely demand that he release her, and expect him to comply, for he would do nothing of the sort!

"I should like to say that I am sorry for what will happen to your reputation but, truth be told, I have no regret in this whatsoever." He shrugged. "I did warn you, Lady Patience, did I not?"

"You expect that I will stay here, simply because you have asked it of me?" Aware that her voice was still shaking, Patience lifted her chin and tried to look at him with a steadiness in her gaze that she did not truly feel. "I will do nothing of the sort."

Lord Newforth let out a mirthless laugh.

"You do not have a choice, Lady Patience! You are to be kept in this room for as long as I deem it necessary. You can see how simple it was for me to have that note sent to you, how the hackney driver waited for you. It will not be difficult in the least to keep you in this room, while I return to London... or mayhap I shall make my way to Bath now, given that everyone now believes that it is where I am."

Closing her eyes, Patience shuddered violently, only to hear Lord Newforth laugh again, this time, the sound coming as a response to her fear. Tears began to burn behind her eyes, but she did not let them fall, knowing that they would do no good. She still had hope, she reminded herself. Her maid had escaped, had run from the hackney, and gone, she trusted, directly to Lord Hastings' townhouse.

"There is no reason for you to behave in this way," she said, her voice rasping. "The only reason you are doing so is because of some misplaced anger over Lord Hastings' refusal to permit you to wed his sister."

"How dare you?" Patience's eyes flew open just as Lord Newforth strode across the room towards her, his eyes narrowed, his face growing hot. "You speak of something you know nothing about," he continued, one hand reaching out for her, grabbing her arm and squeezing it painfully as he shook her, hard. "There was no reason for him to refuse me. No reason at all! I am a gentleman of honor, with enough of a fortune to keep her contented."

"No, you are not." Despite his actions, and despite the fear which ran through her as she spoke, Patience did not hold herself back. "A gentleman of honor would not do such a thing as this. I know of your reputation, and I can well understand why Lord Hastings would refuse you." As Lord Newforth went very still, Patience took another breath and then shook her head, forcing herself to speak without hesitation. "And I think it was right for him to do so. I am glad that your plans for Isabella were foiled. Is it not so that everything you have done thus far has failed completely and utterly?" She tried to smile, despite the pain his tight grip was causing her. "What gives you any confidence that this dark intention of yours will not fail also? I have every confidence that your plan will bring you nothing but mortification and shame; the very opposite of what it is that you desire."

Lord Newforth reeled back, his eyes wide as though she

had stabbed him with a sharp, pointed implement, only to reach one hand back and then strike it hard across her face. Patience let out a cry of pain and fright and pressed one hand to her cheek as Lord Newforth began to roar at her, his words so loud and furious, she could not make them out. Her ears were ringing, her heart thumping frantically as the furious figure of Lord Newforth filled her vision.

Run.

Her eyes strayed to the door behind Lord Newforth. He had pushed her into the room and followed in after her, blocking her escape, but now, in his upset and anger, he had moved closer to her and was further away from the door. Patience stepped back from him all the more, her eyes darting from one place to the next in the room, wondering what she might use to prevent Lord Newforth from following her. If she ran, then he would very quickly catch her, would very easily grab hold of her again, and throw her back into this room. Then, would he not seek to make her even more secure within this place, knowing that she had already once tried to escape?

There.

Her heart skipped in her chest as her gaze fell upon the poker by the fireplace. Dare she do such a thing? Dare she be bold enough to reach for it, to use it to defend herself before making her escape?

It might be the only way.

Her maid could have gone to Lord Hastings' townhouse and found him absent if, that was, she had even managed to reach the townhouse yet. She might now be searching for him, knowing that every minute that passed left Patience in more danger. Even if he was now on his way towards her, Lord Hastings would not be easily able to find where she was, for the street was filled with the entrances to alleyways, with doors that opened to different places – and she might be in any one of them! Patience backed away a little more, making for the fireplace as best she could while Lord Newforth followed her, continuing to scream words of fury at her, his face now purple with anger.

And then, in one swift movement, Patience bent, picked up the poker, and swung it as hard as she could. It struck Lord Newforth across the side of the head, making him bellow with pain and drop to his knees, his hand going to his head – but Patience did not hesitate. Her breathing coming in quick gasps and the poker still in her hand, she rushed for the door, narrowly avoiding Lord Newforth's grasping hand, which reached out to grab at her ankles. Flinging open the door which, mercifully, had not been locked, Patience turned the way she had been brought in, hurrying towards the door and to the outside world. Another cry of rage met her ears, chasing her out of the door as she dragged in air. Her heart clamoring in her chest, she twisted to the right, her feet slipping a little on the cobbled streets.

"Patience!" A cry of fright escaped her as her name was called, sure now that Lord Newforth had recovered himself and was hurrying after her. There did not seem to be anyone else near her, no other person walking through the streets and, even if there had been, Patience was not certain that anyone would have helped her. "Patience, stop!" Her vision blurred as her breathing grew shallow, her fright biting down hard at her strength and pulling it away from her. Her legs wobbled, but still she pressed on, not sure where she was going, but desperate to put as much distance between herself and Lord Newforth. "Patience, wait, please!" It was the *please* that gave her pause. Her strength gone, she staggered to a stop, turning her head as she pulled in air, one hand going to the wall as she fought to keep her balance, her other hand still grasping the poker. "It is I." The familiar face of Lord Hastings came into view as Patience blinked rapidly to clear her vision. "I have found you."

With a cry of relief, Patience dropped the poker and practically fell into his arms, tears now beginning to fall as she felt his arms tight around her, holding her close, promising her that all would be well. Sobs tore through her frame as the fear that had clung to her for so long finally faded away to nothing, leaving her trembling and weak.

"The maid told me where you were," he said, his voice close to her ear. "I came at once. I must hope that Lord Milthorpe has been able to stop Lord Newforth from chasing you."

Patience looked up at him, her breathing growing a little calmer now that she was safe in his arms.

"He is here too?"

"He was with me when the maid came in search of me," he said, releasing her gently, as though he was afraid that, should he do it too quickly, she might collapse. "Are you all right, Patience?" He looked down at her, his eyes searching hers. "Did he hurt you?"

Patience, recalling the slap, closed her eyes for a moment.

"He struck me when I told him that he would not succeed in his endeavor, that he would do nothing but fail, as he had done every other time. My words made him utterly furious. But I struck *him* with the poker to escape, so I think that he may have had the more difficult and painful injury."

Lord Hastings' eyes rounded.

"You did?"

"I had to escape." Patience pulled herself close to him

again. "His threats were very great, and I found myself deeply afraid. I was not afraid of what would happen to me, but more of what would happen to you. I feared for Isabella's happiness, for her future, and for the reputation of all of you."

Lifting his hands, Lord Hastings cupped her face gently, gazing tenderly into her eyes.

"You become more precious to me every day, Patience," he told her, his words burning into her heart and chasing away the last lingering tendrils of fear. "You think of others over yourself, even when a heavy threat is against you. I would have stood by you no matter what was said, however. I hope that you know that."

Patience nodded.

"I do."

"Then let me take you home," he murmured, putting one arm around her shoulders. "And then, I shall return to deal with Lord Newforth."

With a small shake of her head, Patience looked up into his eyes.

"Let me stay."

Lord Hastings' eyebrows lifted.

"You would be willing to be in his company again? Even after everything that he has just done to you?"

"I will not pretend that the thought of looking into his face again is a pleasurable one, but it must be done." Patience squeezed her eyes shut tight for a long moment, then with a long breath, steadied herself and gave him a nod. "I want to be there. I want him to see that he *has* failed, just as I said he would, for you *did* come for me, you *did* keep me from him."

"Only because you escaped first," Lord Hastings told her, before pressing a kiss to her temple. "Very well, my dear. If you are sure that you wish it, then I will take you with me." He gave her another searching look and Patience nodded again to confirm to him that she was ready. "Your strength is yet another reason for me to admire you, my dear lady." Lord Hastings smiled and then let his hand drop to her waist. "Come, then. Let us go."

CHAPTER SEVENTEEN

Despite the smile on his lips, Daniel felt nothing but a bubbling anger beneath. He kept his arm tightly around Patience, walking back the way that he had come, and praying that Lord Milthorpe had been able to secure Lord Newforth.

Recalling how the maid had practically flung herself into his drawing room, Daniel went hot all over, remembering how he had been indignant with the maid, and had tried to demand that she leave the room at once. The butler had followed in after her, apologetic and determined to fetch the maid back again. Had it not been for Lord Milthorpe's interruption, then Daniel might never have heard what the maid had come to tell him. Lord Milthorpe had been the one to give Daniel pause, to suggest that they listen to the lady, given the state of her upset, and thus, with frustration still brewing within him, he had done so. That frustration had quickly turned to fright, and then to fear, as he had practically run from the room, tearing down the hallway and into Lord Milthorpe's waiting carriage. Lord Milthorpe and the maid had followed closely behind, and, within moments, they had begun the drive to where Patience was now being held by Lord Newforth. The maid had, thankfully, known the name of the street they were to go to, having discovered it from the hackney driver she had used to take her to Daniel's townhouse. Daniel had fought against his rising fear as the hackney made its way there, fearing for Patience, for what he would discover when he reached there, and praying that Lord Newforth would have done nothing to ruin her.

Sweat broke out on his forehead as he glanced at the waiting carriage, remembering the moment that he had leaped from it, seeing Patience running as hard as she could down the street with Lord Newforth following her – though, for whatever reason, his steps had been slow and stumbling. He recognized now that it had been the strike of the poker against his head that would have caused such a thing, finding himself almost a little glad that the fellow had been himself caused pain, given all that he had intended to do. Rushing after Patience as he had done – and hearing Lord Milthorpe shout that *he* would get to Lord Newforth – Daniel's heart had ached for her, desperate for her to turn and see that it was he who called for her, not Lord Newforth. The moment she had done so, he had seen abject relief on her face and, hurrying to her, Daniel had wanted nothing more than to pull her into his arms. She had practically fallen into him and, as he had held her tightly against him, Daniel had silently sworn that he would never let her go from his side again.

"Are you sure that you wish to do this?" Looking down at Patience, Daniel took in the whiteness of her cheeks, aware of just how much she needed to have his arm around her at the present moment. "You need not, Patience."

Her blue eyes caught his.

"I want to."

With a nod, Daniel set his shoulders and then walked towards Lord Milthorpe who was standing in the doorway of what appeared to be a somewhat dilapidated house.

"Milthorpe? Where is he?"

"Inside." Lord Milthorpe jerked his head in the direction of the door. "I thought that he must have come from this place, for the door was wide open. Lord Newforth was not particularly difficult to catch, given the injury to his head and thus, I led him back to this place without concern. He is now resting in the small room inside."

"Resting?" Catching the twist of Lord Milthorpe's lips, Daniel lifted one eyebrow. "I can hardly think that he is doing such a thing willingly."

"Oh, he is not." Lord Milthorpe chuckled darkly. "The door to the room within had a key. I now have it in my possession." So saying, he pulled a key out of his pocket and dangled it between thumb and finger. "Do you wish to speak with him?"

Daniel glanced again at Patience but choosing not to ask her again if she truly wished to do this, nodded.

"I think we should all go in."

Lord Milthorpe nodded.

"Very well. Then come with me."

With trepidation in every step, Daniel followed Lord Milthorpe, wondering just how angry Lord Newforth would be, and what he might do because of it. Would they open the door to a furious whirlwind of a man? Would he try to break through them all and escape? Daniel gritted his teeth. He had no intention of letting Lord Newforth go anywhere.

"If you are quite ready?"

With a nod in answer to Lord Milthorpe's question,

Daniel kept his arm tight around Patience as Lord Milthorpe went on to open the door. Pushing it back, he stepped inside, leaving Daniel and Patience to follow, and Daniel did not hesitate.

Lord Newforth, however, did not come rushing at them as Daniel had expected. Instead, he was sitting on the only chair in the dank, dirty room, his jaw jutting forward and fire burning in his eyes. His gaze, however, did not linger on Daniel, but instead turned to Patience.

"*You* did this to me!" So saying, he pulled a bloodied handkerchief away from the side of his head and then gestured to it with the other. "*You!*"

Daniel opened his mouth to retort, only for Lady Patience to answer. With a shrug, she tilted her head and looked at Lord Newforth, a calmness in her which astonished Daniel utterly.

"I hardly think that you can blame me for it, Lord Newforth. After all, you did attempt to kidnap me, and intended to hold me here, in this room, until the entirety of the *ton* thought that I had eloped with another gentleman or some such thing." She shrugged. "I did warn you that you would fail. I confess that I am surprised that you did not listen to me, for I spoke the truth."

Lord Newforth's lip curled.

"Do not think that you have succeeded, Hastings." His eyes turned to Daniel, dark pools of fury that threatened to drown Daniel. "I will never give up. You will suffer the consequences of refusing me your sister's hand."

Daniel shook his head, aware that all of Lord Newforth's threats, his desire to have Daniel suffer, came from a sense of mortification, fury, and bloody-mindedness. He had taken Daniel's refusal as a personal insult – and now required Daniel's punishment in whatever form Lord Newforth wished.

"You are a fool, Newforth." He spoke quite calmly but with great emphasis. "Do you truly think that wasting your time in pursuing me in this manner, given how many times you have failed, is worth your while?"

Lord Newforth shook one finger in Daniel's direction.

"Ah, but I *shall* succeed! No matter what it is that you think to do to me, I shall never give up! Not until the insult has been repaid."

"Refusing you his sister was no insult," Lord Milthorpe began, only for Daniel to hold up one hand, silencing his friend. Releasing Patience gently, he took a few steps closer, a settled determination in his chest.

"You are not a gentleman of any worth," he said, quite calmly. "I did not insult you by refusing you my sister's hand, for you bring such insults upon yourself by your own behavior! Is it not right for me to care for her, more than I would think of *you,* and what upset you might take from my refusal?" When Lord Newforth said nothing, Daniel shook his head. "You have barely any fortune left of your own, Lord Newforth. You have a wrath in you that, even now, warns me away from you. There is nothing about your character that would encourage me to even *think* of you as a suitable match for her - and if you wish to take that as personal insult, then I cannot help that."

"But you will suffer the consequences of it."

"I will not." Daniel looked over his shoulder to where Patience stood, waiting. "You have failed, and you will fail again. I have found a happiness here that I am sure you cannot, and will not, ever be able to understand. No matter what it is that you try, then ultimately, you will fail."

Lord Newforth scoffed at this, pressing the handkerchief back to the side of his head.

"Your reputation, one way or another, will be ruined, and with that, your happiness. You will have to remove from society and never set foot in it again!"

A quiet laugh from behind Daniel made Lord Newforth's scowl return in an instant, darker than Daniel had seen it before.

"Oh, Lord Newforth, you must have a very poor understanding of what happiness is." Continuing to speak, Patience made her way towards Daniel, taking his hand in hers, though her gaze was fixed on Lord Newforth. "Happiness does not come from having a pristine reputation. Nor does it come from being a part of society! What you did not know is that Lord Hastings has desired to remove himself from society ever since you attempted to force his hand and thus, it will not be any trouble to him – or to me, for that matter." Turning her head, she looked up at Daniel, her eyes shining with a brightness that Daniel knew came from within her heart, for he felt it too. "That is why we say you shall fail, Lord Newforth. Even if you do all that you can to bring our reputation into the dirt, our happiness in what we have found in one another will remain. It will be steadfast, no matter what else assails us." Looking back at Lord Newforth, she lifted her shoulders lightly and then let them fall. "Even if you had secured me in this place for many days as you wished, even if the whispers about me had swirled through London, Lord Hastings would not have abandoned me."

"Never." Daniel put one arm about her waist again, seeing how Lord Newforth began to blink rather quickly, his gaze darting from Daniel to Patience to Lord Milthorpe and back again. It was as if he had never even thought of such a scenario, where he might succeed in his efforts but, at the same time, ultimately fail.

"And I can say the same about myself and Isabella." Lord Milthorpe smiled as Daniel threw him a glance. "I would never abandon her, would never turn away from her, no matter what you tried to do to Lord Hastings and the standing of his family name." He let out a wry laugh. "Not only are you poor in funds, Lord Newforth, but it seems that you are also poor in happiness, in friends, and in genuine affection. And that shall be your heavy burden to carry for as long as you choose to bear it."

A sudden thought came shooting into Daniel's mind as Lord Milthorpe spoke.

Poor in funds?

He caught his breath, seeing Patience look at him with wide eyes, perhaps wondering what had made him respond so.

And then, Daniel spoke.

"Though, that being said, I do not much like what it is that you have tried to do to my family and now, to my betrothed," he said, as Lord Newforth turned his head away. "This shall come to an end, Lord Newforth. You will not pursue us any longer in this manner. Lady Winters, it seems, has abandoned you, and brought her efforts to an end, given the failure of her attempt to be of aid to you. Thus, I think that you shall have to follow suit."

Lord Newforth threw himself to his feet, his face quickly turning a shade of crimson.

"Never," he grated, his eyes narrowed slits. "I shall *never–*"

"I think you shall." Daniel cleared his throat and broke into Lord Newforth's retort. "For do you not recall that you owe me a great deal of money?"

This made Lord Newforth stop short. The color in his face began to fade as his eyes rounded, staring back at Daniel as Daniel smiled quietly.

"Lord Newforth owes you money?" Patience asked, as Daniel nodded. "How can that be?"

"I have only just remembered it," Daniel confessed, feeling a little embarrassed. "With all that has happened, it quite went from my mind. But yes, before Lord Newforth even came to speak to me about Isabella, he and I played cards with a small group of gentlemen." Seeing the way that Lord Newforth took a small step back, Daniel let his lips curve. "You recall now, I think? Yes, it was an evening of cards that lasted a long time, for you were *most* insistent on another game, and then another, gambling more and more and more as you tipped brandy after brandy down your throat."

A small, choked sound came from Lord Newforth's lips.

"I have the vowel you gave me," Daniel continued, a sense of relief sweeping through him as he recognized that, finally, he had the upper hand. "A vowel which was taken to the Jerusalem room, if I recall correctly?" Knowing that this meant the vowel was a legal debt, and one that Lord Newforth could not escape from, Daniel's spirits lifted as Lord Newforth shrank back. "I think that I require it to be fulfilled, Lord Newforth."

The gentleman shook his head.

"I – I cannot."

"But you must. You will lose all honor if you do not... and if you cannot pay the debt, then I shall be forced to inform society of it." Daniel's jaw tightened as a flash of anger broke in him again, recalling all that Lord Newforth had done. "You have used society for your own ends, Lord Newforth, and I now do the same. Pay me what you owe, or all shall know of your debt and your shame. Then you shall see just how many of them listen to you as you try to demean my name and reputation."

Lord Newforth opened his mouth to say something, but could only stammer, his brow furrowing, his eyes jumping from place to place as he sought a response, but nothing came out. With a deep breath, Daniel turned on his heel and, taking Patience with him, walked from the room.

"It is over," he said quietly, leading her out of the dark room and back to the light outside. "He can do nothing now. If he dares speak ill of me, then I shall show the *ton* my vowel and that will be enough for them to surmise the reason for his actions."

"And if he does not pay you?"

Daniel led her back towards the carriage.

"I care not about the money. I want him to fade away, to move himself back from society, and from us, so that I need not ever think of him again." Releasing her so that she might climb up into the carriage. "I have all that I need, Patience. And I have it all in you."

EPILOGUE

"I think it has been a wonderful evening."
Patience nodded and smiled, watching as Eleanor danced with Lord Thornlake, a gentleman who had been paying a little more attention to her of late.

"It has been, yes." She smiled at her sister. "And I now see Lord Hurrelton coming to seek you out, my dear sister."

Watching as Christina's cheeks flushed, Patience's smile grew, though she quickly took a few steps away to permit her sister to speak with the gentleman alone.

Letting out a slow breath, Patience felt contentment settle deep within her. At her request, nothing had been said to her mother or sister about what had taken place, though she had been required to share it all with Eleanor, simply so that her cousin could confirm that yes, Patience had been in her company that afternoon. Eleanor had been quite horrified, of course, but all had come to a pleasing conclusion, for Lord Newforth had not been seen in some days now, with the last rumors being that he had returned to his estate, rather than coming back to London. Isabella's betrothal ball had been a marvelous success, and now all that was left for Patience was to look forward to her wedding to the gentleman she had come to care for so very deeply.

"There you are."

Patience turned quickly, only to giggle as Lord Hastings pulled her back into the shadows at the edge of the ballroom, his eyes twinkling and a broad smile on his lips as he did so.

"I know that I ought not to do such a thing, since we are not yet wed, but I could not help it." Putting his arms around her, he looked down into her eyes and held her gaze for a long moment. "My goodness, Patience, you are more beautiful every time I look upon you."

Patience reached up one hand and brushed her fingers lightly across his cheek.

"You are all the more handsome also."

That, she knew, was quite true, for in setting all that Lord Newforth had done behind them, there had come a new freedom, a new joy, into Lord Hastings' character. He smiled more brightly, spoke with more delight, and no longer hid himself in the shadows though, Patience knew, he was still fully resolved to move away from society once they were wed.

"Are you quite well, my dear?" Lord Hastings' expression suddenly became a little more serious. "You are enjoying the evening, I hope?"

"Of course I am. Though," Patience continued, tilting her head a little, "I could do with more time beside you. I miss you when you have to step away."

A soft smile tipped up the edges of his lips.

"As I miss you," he murmured, shifting his feet so that he stood even closer to her. "Patience, my heart cannot help but cry out in agony whenever we are apart, my whole being crying out to come back to be beside you. I count the days until we finally become husband and wife so that I might never be away from you again."

Patience's heart soared at his tender words. They had shared many conversations these last few days, but none had expressed such intimacies before.

"I dream about the day that I am to make my promises to you, Hastings," she said, a sudden tension in her frame as she fought to find the strength to speak the truth of her heart. "I – I am quite in love with you, you know."

Lord Hastings said nothing. He did not look surprised, nor did he frown. Instead, the smile on his lips only grew, a joy in his expression which made Patience let out a breath of relief, seeing now that he too felt the same way as she did.

"My love," he murmured, lifting her hand to his lips, sending a wave of warmth cascading over her. "Yet again, you have the strength that I ought to have possessed. I have not wanted to overwhelm you when there has been so much for you to recover from, but I see now that I ought not to have waited." Lowering her hand, he pressed her fingers gently. "I love you with all of my heart, Patience. You are the most remarkable, wonderful, beautiful, and extraordinary creature that I have ever met, and to have you as my betrothed is so utterly overwhelming, I find myself wondering what I did to deserve such joy. For that is what you are, Patience, you are a joy that fills every part of my heart, every part of my life, and for which I shall always be grateful."

He kissed her there, even as the ball went on around them. His lips were tender, his arms gentle around her. It was as though her very heart was dancing with sheer happiness, as though her whole body was singing with the delight that now filled her.

The darkness of the past had fled from them both and now, as Patience melted into Lord Hastings' arms, all she could see was light, happiness, and love being laid out before her.

It was more than she had ever dreamed of, more than she had ever wanted for herself. As their kiss lingered, Patience willingly lost herself in Lord Hastings' embrace, knowing that their love would last forever, tying their hearts together.

PATIENCE WAS PATIENT! So glad she found someone who would appreciate her!

Did you miss the first book in the Whispers of the Ton series? Check out The Truth about the Earl in the Kindle store!

READ ahead for an excerpt from The Truth about the Earl!

MY DEAR READER

Thank you for reading and supporting my books! I hope this story brought you some escape from the real world into the always captivating Regency world. A good story, especially one with a happy ending, just brightens your day and makes you feel good! If you enjoyed the book, would you leave a review on Amazon? Reviews are always appreciated.

Below is a complete list of all my books! Why not click and see if one of them can keep you entertained for a few hours?

The Duke's Daughters Series
The Duke's Daughters: A Sweet Regency Romance Boxset
A Rogue for a Lady
My Restless Earl
Rescued by an Earl
In the Arms of an Earl
The Reluctant Marquess (Prequel)

A Smithfield Market Regency Romance
The Smithfield Market Romances: A Sweet Regency Romance Boxset
The Rogue's Flower
Saved by the Scoundrel
Mending the Duke
The Baron's Malady

The Returned Lords of Grosvenor Square
The Returned Lords of Grosvenor Square: A Regency Romance Boxset
The Waiting Bride
The Long Return
The Duke's Saving Grace
A New Home for the Duke

The Spinsters Guild
The Spinsters Guild: A Sweet Regency Romance Boxset
A New Beginning
The Disgraced Bride
A Gentleman's Revenge
A Foolish Wager
A Lord Undone

Convenient Arrangements
Convenient Arrangements: A Regency Romance Collection
A Broken Betrothal
In Search of Love
Wed in Disgrace
Betrayal and Lies
A Past to Forget
Engaged to a Friend

Landon House
Landon House: A Regency Romance Boxset
Mistaken for a Rake
A Selfish Heart
A Love Unbroken
A Christmas Match
A Most Suitable Bride

An Expectation of Love

Second Chance Regency Romance
Second Chance Regency Romance Boxset
Loving the Scarred Soldier
Second Chance for Love
A Family of her Own
A Spinster No More

Soldiers and Sweethearts
Soldiers and Sweethearts Boxset
To Trust a Viscount
Whispers of the Heart
Dare to Love a Marquess
Healing the Earl
A Lady's Brave Heart

Ladies on their Own: Governesses and Companions
Ladies on their Own Boxset
More Than a Companion
The Hidden Governess
The Companion and the Earl
More than a Governess
Protected by the Companion

Lost Fortunes, Found Love
Lost Fortunes, Found Love Boxset
A Viscount's Stolen Fortune
For Richer, For Poorer
Her Heart's Choice
A Dreadful Secret
Their Forgotten Love
His Convenient Match

Only for Love
Only for Love : A Clean Regency Boxset
The Heart of a Gentleman
A Lord or a Liar
The Earl's Unspoken Love
The Viscount's Unlikely Ally
The Highwayman's Hidden Heart
Miss Millington's Unexpected Suitor

Waltzing with Wallflowers
The Wallflower's Unseen Charm
The Wallflower's Midnight Waltz
Wallflower Whispers
The Ungainly Wallflower
The Determined Wallflower
The Wallflower's Secret (Revenge of the Wallflowers series)
The Wallflower's Choice

Whispers of the Ton
The Truth about the Earl
The Truth about the Rogue
The Truth about the Marquess
The Truth about the Viscount

Christmas in London Series
The Uncatchable Earl
The Undesirable Duke

Christmas Kisses Series
Christmas Kisses Box Set
The Lady's Christmas Kiss
The Viscount's Christmas Queen
Her Christmas Duke

Christmas Stories
Love and Christmas Wishes: Three Regency Romance Novellas
A Family for Christmas
Mistletoe Magic: A Regency Romance
Heart, Homes & Holidays: A Sweet Romance Anthology

Happy Reading!
　　All my love,
　　Rose

A SNEAK PEEK OF THE TRUTH ABOUT THE EARL

PROLOGUE

"I was very sorry to hear of the death of your husband."

Lady Norah Essington gave the older lady a small smile, which she did not truly feel. "I thank you. You are very kind." Her tone was dull but Norah had no particular concerns as regarded either how she sounded or how she appeared to the lady. She was, yet again, alone in the world, and as things stood, was uncertain as to what her future would be.

"You did not care for him, I think."

Norah's gaze returned to Lady Gillingham's with such force, the lady blinked in surprise and leaned back a fraction in her chair.

"I mean no harm by such words, I assure you. I –"

"You have made an assumption, Lady Gillingham, and I would be glad if you should keep such notions to yourself." Norah lifted her chin but heard her voice wobble. "I should prefer to mourn the loss of my husband without whispers or gossip chasing around after me."

Lady Gillingham smiled, reached forward, and settled one hand over Norah's. "But of course."

Norah turned her head, trying to silently signal that the meeting was now at an end. She was not particularly well acquainted with the lady and, as such, would be glad of her departure so that she might sit alone and in peace. Besides which, if Lady Gillingham had been as bold as to make such a claim as that directly to Norah herself, then what would she think to say to the *ton*? Society might be suddenly full of whispers about Norah and her late husband—and then what would she do?

"I have upset you. Forgive me."

Norah dared a glance at Lady Gillingham, taking in the gentle way her eyes searched Norah's face and the small, soft smile on her lips. "I do not wish you to disparage my late husband, Lady Gillingham. Nor do I want to hear such rumors being spread in London – whenever it would be that I would have cause to return."

"I quite understand, and I can assure you I do not have any intention of speaking of any such thing to anyone in society."

"Then why state such a thing in my presence? My husband is only a sennight gone and, as I am sure you are aware, I am making plans to remove myself to his estate."

"Provided you are still welcome there."

Norah closed her eyes, a familiar pain flashing through her heart. "Indeed." Suddenly, she wanted very much for Lady Gillingham to take her leave. This was not at all what she had thought would occur. The lady, she had assumed, would simply express her sympathies and take her leave.

"Again, I have injured you." Lady Gillingham let out a long sigh and then shook her head. "Lady Essington, forgive me. I am speaking out of turn and with great thoughtlessness, which I must apologize for. The truth is, I come here out of genuine concern for you, given that I have been in the very same situation."

Norah drew her eyebrows together. She was aware that Lady Gillingham was widowed but did not know when such a thing had taken place.

"I was, at that time, given an opportunity which I grasped at with both hands. It is a paid position but done most discreetly."

Blinking rapidly, Norah tried to understand what Lady Gillingham meant. "I am to be offered employment?" She shook her head. "Lady Gillingham, that is most kind of you but I assure you I will be quite well. My husband often assured me his brother is a kind, warm-hearted gentleman and I have every confidence that he will take care of me." This was said with a confidence Norah did not truly feel but given the strangeness of this first meeting, she was doing so in an attempt to encourage Lady Gillingham to take her leave. Her late husband had, in fact, warned her about his brother on more than one occasion, telling her he was a selfish, arrogant sort who would not care a jot for anyone other than himself.

"I am very glad to hear of it, but should you find yourself in any difficulty, then I would beg of you to consider this. I have written for the paper for some time and find myself a little less able to do so nowadays. The truth is, Lady Essington, I am a little dull when it comes to society and very little takes place that could be of any real interest to anyone, I am sure."

Growing a little frustrated, Norah spread her hands. "I do not understand you, Lady Gillingham. Perhaps this is not -"

"An opportunity to *write*, Lady Essington." Lady

Gillingham leaned forward in her chair, her eyes suddenly dark and yet sparkling at the same time. "To write about society! Do you understand what I mean?"

Norah shook her head but a small twist of interest flickered in her heart. "No, Lady Gillingham. I am afraid I do not."

The lady smiled and her eyes held fast to Norah's. "*The London Chronicle*, as you know, has society pages. I am sure you have read them?"

Norah nodded slowly, recalling the times she and her mother had pored over the society pages in search of news as to which gentlemen might be worth considering when it came to her future. "I have found them very informative."

"Indeed, I am glad to hear so." Lady Gillingham smiled as if she had something to do with the pages themselves. "There is a rather large column within the society pages that mayhap you have avoided if you are averse to gossip and the like."

Norah shifted uncomfortably in her chair. The truth was, she *had* read them many times over and had been a little too eager to know of the gossip and rumors swirling through London society whilst, at the same time, refusing to speak of them to anyone else for fear of spreading further gossip.

"I can see you understand what it is I am speaking about. Well, Lady Essington, you must realize that someone writes such a column, I suppose?" She smiled and Norah nodded slowly. "*I* am that person."

Shock spread through Norah's heart and ice filled her chest. Not all of the gossip she had read had been pleasant – indeed, some of it had been so very unfavorable that reputations had been quite ruined.

"You are a little surprised but I must inform you I have

set a great deal of trust in you by revealing this truth." Lady Gillingham's smile had quite faded and instead, Norah was left with a tight-lipped older lady looking back at her with steel in her dark eyes.

"I – I understand."

"Good." Lady Gillingham smiled but there was no lightness in her expression. "The reason I speak to you so, Lady Essington, is to offer you the opportunity in the very same way that I was all those years ago."

For some moments, Norah stared at Lady Gillingham with undisguised confusion. She had no notion as to what the lady meant nor what she wanted and, as such, could only shake her head.

Lady Gillingham sighed. "I am tired of writing my column, Lady Essington. As I have said, it is a paid position and all done very discreetly. I wish to return to my little house in the country and enjoy being away in the quiet countryside rather than the hubbub of London. The funds I have received for writing this particular column have been more than enough over the years and I have managed to save a good deal so that I might retire to the country in comfort."

"I see." Still a little confused, Norah twisted her lips to one side for a few moments. "And you wish for *me* to write this for you?"

"For yourself!" Lady Gillingham flung her hands in the air. "They want to continue the column, for it is *very* popular, and as such, they require someone to write it. I thought that, since you find yourself in much the same situation as I was some years ago, you might be willing to think on it."

Blowing out a long, slow breath, Norah found herself nodding out but quickly stopped it from occurring. "I think I should like to consider it a little longer."

"But of course. You have your mourning period, and thereafter, perhaps you might be willing to give me an answer?"

Norah frowned. "But that is a little over a year away."

"Yes, I am well aware it is a long time, Lady Essington. But I shall finish writing for this Season in the hope that you will take over thereafter. It is, as I am sure you have been able to tell, quite secretive and without any danger."

Norah gave her a small smile, finding her heart flooding with a little relief. "Because you are Mrs. Fullerton," she answered, as Lady Gillingham beamed at her. "You write as Mrs. Fullerton, I should say."

"Indeed, I do. I must, for else society would not wish to have me join them in anything, and then where would I be?" A murmur of laughter broke from her lips as she got to her feet, bringing her prolonged visit to an end. "Consider what I have suggested, my dear. I do not know what your circumstances are at present and I am quite certain you will *not* be aware of them until you return to the late Lord Essington's estate but I am quite sure you would do excellently. You may, of course, write to me whenever you wish with any questions or concerns that I could answer for you."

"I very much appreciate your concern *and* your consideration, Lady Gillingham." Rising to her feet, Norah gave the lady a small curtsy, which was returned. "I shall take the year to consider it."

"Do." Reaching out, Lady Gillingham grasped Norah's hands and held them tightly, her eyes fixed on Norah's. "Do not permit yourself to be pushed aside, Lady Essington. Certain characters might soon determine that you do not deserve what is written on Lord Essington's will but be aware that it cannot be contested. Take what is yours and make certain you do all you can for your comfort. No one will take from you what is rightfully yours, I assure you."

Norah's smile slipped and she could only nod as Lady Gillingham squeezed her hands. She was rather fearful of returning to her late husband's estate and being informed of her situation as regarded her husband's death.

"And you must promise me that you will not speak of this to anyone."

"Of course," Norah promised without hesitation. "I shall not tell a soul, Lady Gillingham. Of that, you can be quite certain."

"Good, I am glad." With another warm smile, Lady Gillingham dropped Norah's hands and made her way to the door. "Good afternoon, Miss Essington. I do hope your sorrow passes quickly."

Norah nodded and smiled but did not respond. Did Lady Gillingham know Norah had never had a kind thought for her husband? That their marriage had been solely because of Lord Essington's desire to have a young, pretty wife by his side rather than due to any real or genuine care or consideration for her? Telling herself silently that such a thing did not matter, Norah waited until Lady Gillingham had quit the room before flopping back into her chair and blowing out a long breath.

Most extraordinary. Biting her lip, Norah considered what Lady Gillingham had offered her. Was it something she would consider? Would she become the next writer of the *London Chronicle* society column? It was employment, but not something Norah could simply ignore.

"I might very well require some extra coin," she murmured to herself, sighing heavily as another rap came at the door. Most likely, this would be another visitor coming to express their sympathy and sorrow. Whilst Norah did not begrudge them, she was finding herself rather weary.

I have a year to consider, she reminded herself, calling for the footman to come into the room. *One year. And then I may very well find myself as the new Mrs. Fullerton.*

CHAPTER ONE

One year later.
Taking the hand of her coachman, Norah descended from the carriage and drew in a long breath.

I am back in London.

The strange awareness that she was quite alone – without companion or chaperone – rushed over her, rendering Norah a little uncomfortable. Wriggling her shoulders a little in an attempt to remove such feelings from herself, Norah put a smile on her face and began to walk through St James' Park, praying that Lady Gillingham would be waiting as she had promised.

The last year had been something of a dull one and it brought Norah a good deal of pleasure to be back in town. Society had been severely lacking and the only other people in the world she had enjoyed conversation with had been her lady's maid, Cherry, and the housekeeper. Both had seemed to recognize that Norah was a little lonely and as the months had passed, a semblance of friendship – albeit a strange one – had begun to flourish. However, upon her return to town, Norah had been forced to leave both the maid and the housekeeper behind, for she was no longer permitted to reside in the small estate that had been hers for the last year. Now, she was to find a way to settle in London and with an entirely new complement of staff.

"Ah, Lady Essington! I am so glad to see you again."

Lady Gillingham rose quickly from where she had been seated on the small, wooden bench and, much to Norah's surprise, grasped her hands tightly whilst looking keenly into her eyes.

"I do hope you are well?"

Norah nodded, a prickling running down her spine. "I am quite well, I thank you."

"You have been looked after this past year?"

Opening her mouth to say that yes, she was quite satisfied, Norah slowly closed it again and saw the flicker of understanding in Lady Gillingham's eye.

"The newly titled Lord Essington did not wish for me to reside with him so I was sent to the dower house for the last few months," she explained, as Lady Gillingham's jaw tightened. "I believe that Lord Essington has spent the time attempting to find a way to remove from me what my late husband bequeathed but he has been unable to do so."

Lady Gillingham's eyes flared and a small smile touched the corner of her mouth. "I am very glad to hear it."

"I have a residence here in London and a small complement of staff." It was not quite the standard she was used to but Norah was determined to make the best of it. "I do not think I shall be able to purchase any new gowns - although it may be required of me somehow – but I am back in town, at the very least."

Lady Gillingham nodded, turned, and began to walk along the path, gesturing for Norah to fall into step with her. "You were given only a small yearly allowance?"

Norah shrugged one shoulder lightly. "It is more than enough to take care of my needs, certainly."

"But not enough to give you any real ease."

Tilting her head, Norah considered what she said, then chose to push away her pride and nod.

"It is as you say." There would be no additional expenses, no new gowns, gloves, or bonnets and she certainly could not eat extravagantly but at least she had a comfortable home. "The will stated that I was to have the furnished townhouse in London and that my brother-in-law is liable for all repairs to keep it to a specific standard for the rest of my remaining life and that, certainly, is a comfort."

"I can see that it is, although might you consider marrying again?"

Norah hesitated. "It is not something I have given a good deal of thought to, Lady Gillingham. I have had a great deal of loss these last few years, with the passing of my mother shortly after my marriage and, thereafter, the passing of Lord Essington himself. To find myself now back in London without a parent or husband is a little strange, and I confess that I find it a trifle odd. However, for the moment, it is a freedom that I wish to explore rather than remove from myself in place of another marriage."

Lady Gillingham laughed and the air around them seemed to brighten. "I quite understand. I, of course, never married again and there is not always a desire to do so, regardless. That is quite an understandable way of thinking and you must allow yourself time to become accustomed to your new situation."

"Yes, I think you are right."

Tilting her head slightly, Lady Gillingham looked sidelong at Norah. "And have you given any consideration to my proposal?"

Norah hesitated, her stomach dropping. Until this moment, she had been quite determined that she would *not* do as Lady Gillingham had asked, whereas now she was no longer as certain. Realizing she would have to live a somewhat frugal life for the rest of her days *or* marry a gentleman with a good deal more fortune – which was, of course, somewhat unlikely since she was a widow – the idea of earning a little more coin was an attractive one.

"I – I was about to refuse until this moment. But now that I am back in your company, I feel quite changed."

Lady Gillingham's eyes lit up. "Truthfully?"

Letting out a slightly awkward laugh, Norah nodded. "Although I am not certain I shall have the same way with words as you. How do you find such interesting stories?"

The burst of laughter that came from Lady Gillingham astonished Norah to the point that her steps slowed significantly.

"Oh, forgive me, Lady Essington! It is clear you have not plunged the depths of society as I have."

A slow flush of heat crept up Norah's cheeks. "It is true that I was very well protected from any belligerent gentlemen and the like. My mother was most fastidious."

"As she ought." Lady Gillingham attempted to hide her smile but it fought to remain on her lips. "But you shall find society a very different beast now, Lady Essington!"

Norah shivered, not certain that she liked that particular remark.

"You are a widowed lady, free to do as you please and act as you wish. You will find that both the gentlemen and ladies of the *ton* will treat you very differently now and that, Lady Essington, is where you will find all manner of stories being brought to your ears."

"I see."

A small frown pulled at Lady Gillingham's brow. "However, I made certain any stories I wrote had a basis in fact. I do not like to spread rumors unnecessarily. I stayed far from stories that would bring grave injury to certain parties."

Norah nodded slowly, seeing the frown and realizing just how seriously Lady Gillingham had taken her employment.

"There is a severe responsibility that must be considered before you take this on, Lady Essington. You must be aware that whatever you write *will* have consequences."

Pressing her lips together tightly, Norah thought about this for a few moments. "I recall that my mother and I used to read the society papers very carefully indeed, to make certain we would not keep company with any gentlemen who were considered poorly by the *ton*."

Lady Gillingham nodded. "Indeed, that is precisely what I mean. If a lady had been taken advantage of, then I would never write about her for fear of what that might entail. However, I would make mention of the gentleman in question, in some vague, yet disparaging, way that made certain to keep the rest of the debutantes away from him."

"I understand."

"We may not be well acquainted, Lady Essington, but I have been told of your kind and sweet nature by others. I believe they thought very well of your mother and, in turn, of you."

Norah put her hand to her heart, an ache in her throat. "I thank you."

Lady Gillingham smiled softly. "So what say you, Lady Essington? Will you do as I have long hoped?"

"Will I write under the name of Mrs. Fullerton?" A slow, soft smile pulled at her lips as she saw Lady

Gillingham nod. "And when would they wish their first piece?"

Lady Gillingham shrugged. "I write every week about what I have discovered. Sometimes the article is rather long and sometimes it is very short. The amount you write does not matter. It is what it contains that is of interest. They will pay you the same amount, regardless."

"They?" Norah pricked up her ears at the mention of money. "And might I ask how much is being offered?"

Norah's eyes widened as Lady Gillingham told her of the very large amount that would be given to her for every piece written. *That would allow me to purchase one new gown at the very least!*

"And it is the man in charge of the *London Chronicle* that has asked me for this weekly contribution. In time, you will be introduced to him. But that is only if you are willing to take on the role?"

Taking in a deep breath, Norah let it out slowly and closed her eyes for a moment. "Yes, I think I shall."

Lady Gillingham clapped her hands together in delight, startling a nearby blackbird. "How wonderful! I shall, of course, be glad to assist you with your first article. Thereafter, I fully intend to return to my house in the countryside and remain far away from *all* that London society has to offer." Her smile faded as she spoke, sending a stab of worry into Norah's heart. Could it be that after years of writing such articles, of being in amongst society and seeing all that went on, Lady Gillingham was weary of the *ton*? Norah swallowed hard and tried to push her doubts away. This was to bring her a little more coin and, therefore, a little more ease. After all that she had endured these last few years, that would be of the greatest comfort to her.

"So, when are you next to go into society?"

Norah looked at Lady Gillingham. "I have only just come to London. I believe I have an invitation to Lord Henderson's ball tomorrow evening, however."

"As have I." Lady Gillingham looped her arm through Norah's, as though they were suddenly great friends. "We shall attend together and I will help you find not only what you are to write about but I shall also introduce you to various gentlemen and ladies that you might wish to befriend."

A little confused, Norah frowned. "For what purpose?"

"Oh, some gentlemen, in particular, will have *excellent* potential when it comes to your writings. You do not have to like them – indeed, it is best if you do *not*, for your conscience's sake."

Norah's spirits dropped low. Was this truly the right thing for her to be doing? She did not want to injure gentlemen and ladies unnecessarily, nor did she want to have guilt on her conscience. *But the money would be so very helpful.*

"I can choose what I write, yes?"

Lady Gillingham glanced over at her sharply. "Yes, of course."

"And the newspaper will not require me to write any falsehoods?"

Lady Gillingham shook her head. "No, indeed not."

Norah set her shoulders. "Then I shall do as you have done and write what I think is only best for society to know, in order to protect debutantes and the like from any uncouth gentlemen."

"That is fair." Lady Gillingham smiled and Norah took in a long breath, allowing herself to smile as she settled the matter with her conscience. "I am sure you shall do very well indeed, Lady Essington."

Norah tilted her head up toward the sky for a moment as a sense of freedom burst over her once again. "I must hope so, Lady Gillingham. The ball will be a very interesting evening indeed, I am sure."

I THINK the society column will yield some very interesting stories, don't you? I hope Lady Essington does well! Check out the rest of the story in the Kindle Store The Truth about the Earl

JOIN MY MAILING LIST AND FACEBOOK READER GROUP

Sign up for my newsletter to stay up to date on new releases, contests, giveaways, freebies, and deals!

Free book with signup!

Monthly Facebook Giveaways! Books and Amazon gift cards!
Join my reader group on Facebook!

Rose's Ravenous Readers

Facebook Page: https://www.facebook.com/rosepearsonauthor

Website: www.RosePearsonAuthor.com
You can sign up for my Newsletter on my website too!

Follow me on Goodreads: Author Page

Printed in Great Britain
by Amazon